W9-AVQ-921

Bleed

Bleed

Laurie Faria Stolarz

HYPERION ❧ NEW YORK

First Edition
1 3 5 7 9 10 8 6 4 2
Printed in the United States of America
Designed by Elizabeth H. Clark
Library of Congress Cataloging-in-Publication Data on file.
ISBN 0-7868-3854-X (hardcover)
Reinforced binding
Visit www.hyperionbooksforchildren.com

For all who bleed

adorable wisps of short, honey-colored hair that make capital C's and inverted J's at the front and back of his legs. The look-out-*David*, Michelangelo-sculpted cuts.

Him = Sean O'Connell. The one, I truly believe, I was put on this earth to be with, to make real, live soap-opera love with. Except, he's my best friend Kelly's boyfriend. Reason #47 why my life sucks.

He looks more tired than usual today, like the sun has drained all the blood from his body and replaced it with boiling water. I wonder if he's hungry, if I should bring him something to eat.

I edge the curtain open wider and watch the white of his T-shirt wilt to a pale peachy color as sweat drips down from his shoulders and neck. I study the way his teeth pinch his bottom lip each time he looks up toward the sun. His shoulders round forward as he turns the mower away from the house, and the small of his back slopes downward like half of a valentine heart.

After a couple weeks of watching him at the window, I commented to my mother about the Harrises' well-maintained lawn and shrubbery, the perfectly square holly bushes, and how the sidewalk has been shaved of the dandelion patches that used to sprout through the cracks. I suggested that she hire Sean to do our yard, too. But she was able to see through that suggestion, and told me she wasn't ready to throw away good, hard-earned money so I could get chummy with my best friend's boyfriend.

I sit back on my bed and imagine what Sean might want to eat, what I might bring him. A Popsicle? But the juice would probably drip all over my fingers by the time I made it over there. A couple of oatmeal-and-raisin cookies? But those are from a box.

Lucy, my velvety white cat, trots into my room and sits in the square patch the sun has painted on the hardwood floor. I click my tongue for her to come and join me, even kick the bubble of covers down to make room for her on the bed. No deal. I have to resort to force. I snatch her up from the floor and plop her onto my lap, doing my best to scratch at her cheeks the way she likes and rub behind her ears. But she runs off to take her place on the window perch in the living room, like the traitor she is.

The other day I sat on my bed, trying to conjure up a list of all the ways Kelly has betrayed me since we were eight. It took me four whole hours to come up with three instances. I pluck the notebook from beside my bed and flip to the page, mostly filled with doodles of three-dimensional squares, and vines of daisies and roses. I read the occasions of betrayal softly to myself: 1. In fourth grade Kelly slipped a secret-admirer note in my desk at school and signed it with Ricky Malick's name. When I had our friend Maria go up to Ricky's friend Mike at recess, to ask him if Ricky really liked me, Mike snatched the note and read it aloud to everyone in our class. They laughed at me and Ricky, and Ricky never spoke to me again after that. 2. In eighth grade Kelly got asked to the junior-high dance by Billy Ready, the same guy I liked. I knew she knew I liked him, even though I never told her I did. But obviously, my feelings didn't matter, because the two of them ended up going together while I stayed home and played with Lucy.

3. Just last year Kelly told me she'd come with me to get my hair straightened at her favorite hair salon for the sophomore semi. Apparently, her aunt knows someone who works at one of those trendy places on Newbury Street, and Kelly always gets a huge discount. But she blew me off instead. She told me that she had to help her mother clean the house, but I later found out from Maria that she went to the movies with Chuck Wagner, a senior on the soccer team.

Of course, none of these relationships worked out. Kelly only keeps her boyfriends for a few months max— aside from Sean, that is. I think she likes the chase more than anything else. Plus, it's not like she and Sean are going to get married or anything. So they've been going out for eight months—big deal. If she hadn't left to visit her dad, she probably would've broken up with him by now anyway.

I turn another page in the notebook. For every one of Kelly's betrayals on my list, there's an example of when she's been really great. Like the time she stayed up all night on the phone, listening to me cry over how Ferris Beckman dumped me for baton-twirling Monica Piramachi. The time she told Ms. McManus, our history teacher, that the cheat sheet on the floor was hers, not mine, because she was acing history anyway. And the time in seventh grade when she told the school nurse that it was she who needed a maxi pad, *super-absorbency*, because I was too embarrassed to ask.

I've tried to find things to distract myself from all this. Yesterday, I cleaned out my closet and dresser and brought all my old clothes to the Salvation Army deposit box on Canal Street. And earlier today I rearranged my photo albums so they make sense. I took out all the pictures that don't mean anything to me—pictures of my older brother's friends; a picture of a cute boy that came with the frame I'm using to hold my middle-school graduation picture; pictures of my parents' friends' babies, kids I don't even know. Pictures I put in there merely to fill up the pages.

I glance at the snapshot of Kelly and me that I've set aside: the two of us sitting on my front steps, playing War with two decks of cards. I remember how we used to play every Friday night in the summer, just before the sun went down. We'd sip raspberry iced tea and talk about what we would do when we grew up, who we would be. I hold the picture up and glance back toward the window.

Sean is still there.

I drop the photo back on my dresser and adjust the focus on my binoculars. He's so close, like I can reach out and touch the tag sticking out from his shirt, help him by tucking it back in. I imagine doing this for him in the

8

hallway at school. Him thanking me with a kiss, and everyone smiling and tilting their heads at how cute we are.

He shuts the mower off and yanks a rag from the back pocket of his shorts. Sweat drips over his pale eyebrows, along his nose, down his lip, parting his mouth, and then over the moon-shaped cleft in his chin. He swipes the rag over his face and then looks up in my direction. I drop the binoculars to my lap and freeze. At first I pull away, hide behind the curtain so he doesn't see me. But then I feel myself edging back toward the screen, not caring if he does. I think he spots me, and this makes my heart go off at about a thousand decibels, like one of those vibrating clocks that shakes you out of dreamland. But instead he just reaches for the water bottle on the front porch, setting the clock back to snooze mode.

Snooze mode—just like my life.

Sean places his lips over the mouth of the bottle and tilts his head back to get a satisfying drink. I watch the lump of his Adam's apple bob up and down as the water swims down his throat, and feel myself swallow as well.

I rack my brain for just one more example of Kelly's betrayal. But the only one that keeps creeping across my mind is the one I am most afraid to write down. Was Kelly's going after Sean a betrayal? She knew how much I liked him. Knew since the third grade, when I stared at him from behind open phonics books and monkey bars at recess. When I wrote his name a million times inside my notebook covers—*Sean + Nicole, Mrs. Sean O'Connell, Nicole loves Sean 4-eva*—and put it in MASH games that foretold who my husband would be and how many children we'd have.

She knew it when I memorized his class schedule each semester. When I'd sit bundled up at the ice rink watching his hockey games. When, at the beginning of each year, I came up with all these elaborate schemes to try and be his lab partner, or bump into him in the hallway.

Last October was the worst. But I was determined to finally ask Sean out. I had it all planned. The Sadie Hawkins dance was still a few weeks away. I would come home from school, get all my house chores done so my mother wouldn't be on my back, and then call him up and ask him to go with me.

The only wrinkle in my otherwise brilliant scheme: Kelly insisted on coming over that day. She even helped me finish all my chores, right down to peeling the potatoes for our dinner that night despite her recent manicure—*anything*, she said, to get my butt to the dance instead of parked at home in front of the tube, where it'd been during every other social event.

"Okay, I'm really going to do it now," I told her, sitting on the edge of my bed, my heart practically pumping through my chest. I'd been sitting in that exact same spot for more than forty minutes, the phone in one hand, Sean's number pressed in the other.

"Give it up," Kelly groaned, when forty minutes turned

into an hour. "It's obviously not going to happen today."

"I'm *going* to call him," I insisted.

"Uh-huh." She rolled her eyes. "I need a snack. Yo hungry?"

I shook my head and watched as she hopped off th bed and bounded downstairs to the kitchen.

The perfect opportunity to finally do it.

I dialed the numbers quickly and pressed the receiver to my ear.

"Hello?" said a boy's voice—*Sean's* voice, I was so sure.

I opened my mouth to say something back, but all that came out was a soft choking sound.

"Hel-looo?" the voice repeated.

"Is this Sean?" I asked in practically a whisper.

"Yeah. Who's this? Danielle?"

Danielle *who*? I almost hung up, only I heard a weird rustling sound on the other end of the line.

"Not Danielle," Kelly's voice said through the receiver. She'd obviously picked up the phone extension downstairs.

"Then *who*?" Sean asked.

"It's Kelly from school."

My mouth dropped open. The receiver still pressed against my ear, I sprung from the bed and flew down the stairs with the full intent of ripping the phone right out of her meddling little hands. Kelly must have heard me charging, because she ran into the bathroom and locked herself in.

I pounded on the door, but it obviously didn't bother her any, because she kept right on talking to him Completely horrified, I kept listening.

"So what's up?" she asked him.

"Not much," Sean answered.

"Surprised it's me?"

"A little."

"Oh, come on," she continued. "I've seen the way you look at me in history class. Don't deny it."

"Whatever," he said.

"I'm just *kidding*. God . . . can't you take a joke?"

"What do you want?" he asked, trying to get to the point.

"Are you going to the Sadie Hawkins thing or what?"

"I don't know."

"*I don't know* as in you haven't been asked yet?"

"I guess so."

"I guess so *what*? You *haven't* been asked?"

"Not yet; isn't it still a whole month away?"

"Hmm . . . interesting," she said, ignoring the question. "So what do you think of Nicole Bouchard?"

"Who?"

"Nicole Bouchard," she repeated, turning up the volume on her voice.

"I don't know."

"Do you think she's pretty?"

"Kelly!" I hissed, patting on the door, half afraid that he would hear me, more afraid of the damage Kelly

12

could do. "Hang up NOW!" I whisper-shouted.

"What's going on?" Sean demanded. "Who's on the other line?"

"No one," Kelly said, letting out another giggle. "It's just me."

"Yeah, right."

"Are you trying to tell me that you're hearing voices? They have shrinks for that, you know."

"Whatever," Sean said. "I gotta go."

And with that, he hung up.

"Great!" Kelly shouted. "I totally could have gotten you in!" She whipped the bathroom door open and glared at me like his hanging up was *my* fault.

"I can't believe you just did that," I said.

"Are you kidding me? I was trying to do you a favor."

I shook my head and bit my tongue, barely able to even look at her.

"Like it even matters anyway." Kelly sighed. "The guy was a total ass. It was like he didn't even know who you were."

I shrugged, holding myself back from tearing up.

"You need to forget him, Nickie."

"I will," I whispered.

"Good, because it's not like he's even worth it. Sean's so completely average." With that, she hugged me, telling me how I could do *so* much better than Sean O'Connell, how she could get me a date with Ferris Beckman if I wanted, how she knew for a fact that he liked me.

Feeling defeated, I agreed. And then a few weeks later, when me and Ferris didn't work out, Kelly announced that she was going to get Sean *for* me—for real this time.

But instead, she got him for herself. "You're not mad, are you?" she asked, the new-boyfriend excitement on her face masked only partially by concern. "I mean, you know I'd never do anything to hurt you. It's just that you said it yourself—you want to forget about him, right?"

For some reason, I nodded. After that she prattled on about how if it bothered me, she'd call it all off, how she had no idea how it even happened, and that our friendship was *way* more important than some stupid boy. "You know I love you," she said, giving me an extra-tight squeeze.

"I love you, too," I repeated—only I wished I were saying the words to Sean.

"Nicole," my mother yells from somewhere downstairs. "I'm going to the hospital. Are you sure you don't want to volunteer a few hours in the gift shop?"

"No thanks," I yell back. "I've got some stuff to do."

It's eleven thirty. I still have over an hour before I'm supposed to pick up Maria. I decide to go outside, pretend to get the mail or something, peek over and act surprised to see him there. It's summer, for God's sake, and I haven't seen him since the last day of school. He'll want to say hello to someone from school, especially me, Kelly's closest friend. We can even talk about Kelly. That'll be fine. That'll be perfect. I can go over just to find out how Kelly is. I haven't spoken to her in two whole weeks, after all. "I saw you out here working," I practice into the mirror. "By the way, have you heard from Kelly?" I do want to know if she's having a good time. Maybe Sean has some news.

I watch my lips as I practice what I'll say. I hate my lips, the top one is *way* fuller than the bottom. I conceal it as best as I can with more Nude Glow, the way the woman at the Clinique counter advised me. I wish I had lips like Kelly's, stacked up like perfect little peach wedges, lipstick or not.

I'll just go over and say hello, I tell myself, squirting down my hair with extra spray gel. I repeat the word "hello" in my head as I make my way past the mailbox and across the front lawn.

"Sean!" I shout. I raise my right arm up and dip my hips to the left, the way Kelly once did when she spotted me and Maria coming across the school parking lot.

"Hey," he says. "What's up?"

"Not much," I say. "I didn't know you worked for the Harrises."

He nods and runs his fingers through his hair.

"How's your summer going?"

He glances at the lawn. "It's going."

I scour my brain for something to talk about. For all the time I've spent imagining this moment, I feel like I should have a dozen things to say. But somehow, I can't think of one.

15

"Kelly will be home in a few weeks, I guess," he says.

"Yeah, Maria and I are getting together later to start planning a surprise welcome-home party. You'll have to come. To the party, I mean." I twirl a piece of hair and bring it up to my lip for coverage. "Has she called you lately?"

"A couple days ago. She's doing good. Likes having her own pool."

"Is she getting along with her father?"

"I guess so. I don't know. I only talked to her for five minutes. She had to go."

"Yeah, she must be pretty busy. I thought we'd be talking more, you know . . . since she has free nights and weekends on her cell plan. My parents refuse to let me get one, and I know they'd absolutely kill me if I called her in California." A weird gurgling sound escapes my throat when I say California. *Quite* attractive.

Sean shrugs and looks away. So not interested. I imagine what Kelly would do, how she would handle the situation.

"It's so hot out here," I say. "How can you work in this heat?" I grab the front of my shirt and jerk it back and forth from my chest as a fan. I notice Sean peek down at my front, then at the house, then back at my front again.

"I have to. I'm saving up to buy a new car."

"You are? What kind?"

"Jeep."

"Sweet," I say. "Will you take me for a ride sometime?" Yuck—hearing these words trail out my mouth, I decide to come up with some excuse to leave, like having to water the garden.

"Sure," he says. "Anytime."

"Really?"

Maybe Kelly had exaggerated their relationship. I've caught her blowing stuff like this way out of proportion before. Like the time she said she landed a date with Derik captain-of-the-lacrosse-team LaPointe. I later found out that Kelly's mom did business with Derik's parents and, as a thank-you, Derik's dad *made him* take Kelly to a party. *Some* date.

I point a hip toward Sean and churn my hands on the mower handle, like revving a motorcycle engine. "Looks pretty good." I make an effort to glance at the lawn, but end up staring at those calves. I can't believe I am this close to them.

"I'll say," he says.

I peek up at him and he's just . . . staring at me. Calm down, I tell myself, looking away, practically biting through my bottom lip. Think. What would Kelly do?

"You must be dying out here in this heat," I say finally. I check my hair to make sure it hasn't kinkified on me, wishing I had thick and wavy locks like the Pantene girl, or straight, Barbie doll–blond tresses like Kelly.

"It does get pretty hot."

I pull up on my shirt to expose my tan belly, the way Kelly did once at this college rush party she made us crash, so she could nab a guy from Zeta House—like Zeta House even means anything when you're a sophomore in high school.

"Get out!" Sean says. "You have a navel ring. Kelly never told me that."

I thread the silver loop, pierced into my navel, with my pinkie finger and smile with pressed lips, the way I did in my sophomore class portrait, when everyone told me I looked so sweet. I got the navel ring with Kelly. She dared me, saying I was way too pure to actually go through with it. "I bet there's a lot Kelly hasn't told you about me."

"Oh, yeah? Like what?"

I stare at him a few seconds, considering the situation and what I should do. Maybe I'm doing Kelly a favor. Maybe she wants to break things off with him. Maybe if she really cared anything about him, she wouldn't have left him for a whole summer, wouldn't have run three thousand miles away from him.

"For example," I say, not able to hide my lip in the smile, "did she tell you I have an inground swimming pool?"

He shakes his head and wipes the sweat from his forehead with a dry patch of T-shirt. With him lifting his shirt up this way, I'm able to see the tiny golden hairs that make a woven stripe right below his navel.

"Well I do," I say. "It's in the shape of a giant curly S." I tug the strap of my bathing suit out from my shirt and allow it to snap back into place. *Ouch!* "That's where

I'm going right now." I pick his water bottle up from the stairs and place its coolness on my cheeks, forehead, and also at my neck, the way they do it in sexy cola commercials. Then I take a sip. "Feel like taking a dunk?"

I almost catch a glimpse of a quivering lip, but he bites it just in time. "I really need to finish up my work," he says. "Maybe another time."

"Sure." I hand him back the water bottle, and the squeeze of my grip causes water to shoot out of the straw. *So* smooth. "Sorry," I say.

"Don't worry about it." He wipes the squirt from his face. "Just water."

"I guess I'll see you around." As I walk away I can feel the heat of his stare press against the back of my thighs, the tanned small of my back where my shorts meet my top, and my hips as they sway from side to side, catwalk style. Before taking a turn into my backyard, I stop to glance back at him, just to check if he's still there, watching.

He is.

I walk around the edge of the pool and dip a foot in to test the temperature. The water sparkles up at me, the surface flashing like tiny white Christmas lights. I peel the sweat-dampened clothes from my bubble gum–pink tank-ini bathing suit, the top of which is supposed to help create the illusion of bigger boobs. I toss the clothes to the side and imagine Sean's expression as they fall to his feet.

But when I look back, I'm alone.

I position myself on the diving board and aim my body toward the center like a dart. Not too much splash—the right amount—a sound that would make any neighbor jealous. I swim underwater toward the deep end, telling myself that by the time I reach the end, Sean will be there, waiting for me.

He isn't.

I paddle around on the raft for almost an hour, allowing my arms and the back of my neck to crisp and redden from the sun. Staring down at my reflection wavering back and forth in the water, I can make out my frizzy hair (wet or not), my pudgy upper lip, and through it all I can see the maze of dirt at the bottom of the pool from my filthy bare feet. I'll have to vacuum before my mother gets home and sees.

I rest my head on the raft, and my bangs block the sun from my eyes. I feel stupid and embarrassed. Who am I to invite Sean O'Connell to join me in the pool? I'm not anybody. Not Kelly with her good looks. Not Maria with her nerves of steel.

I remember this one time when Maria, Kelly, and I went to a party in the next town over. Maria had been playing eye-tag with this cute college boy all night. Pissed that he hadn't actually approached her by eleven o'clock, she stormed her way over to him and said all of three words: "Top or bottom?" I don't remember what his answer was. All I remember is the sight of his clunker

Camaro bopping up and down in the supermarket parking lot across the street.

Not that I would ever want to be like Maria in that way. Sometimes I think if it weren't for Kelly, Maria and I probably wouldn't even be friends. It's just . . . it would be nice to have her I-don't-care-what-anyone-else-thinks attitude for at least one full day—to be able to take and do whatever it is I want, and not have to worry about the consequences.

I take a deep breath and paddle over to the ladder, wondering if Sean will tell Kelly that I invited him over. I decide I should go back inside, put on some dry clothes, and go pick up Maria, so we can start planning for Kelly's welcome-home. I should even e-mail Kelly later, tell her I really do miss her, and can't wait until she gets back. I'll send along that picture of us playing double-deck War so she can keep it by her bed.

I step one foot on the bottom rung of the ladder, and that's when I hear it. *Him.* His voice. In *my* yard.

"Is that invitation still good?" he asks.

I turn around and there he is, standing only a few feet away, by the fence, turning my skin to absolute gooseflesh.

"Hi," he says.

I have no idea how to answer him or what to say. I just stare at him, my mouth hanging open, like I'm the biggest dork *ever*. I realize I'm doing this, and that only makes it worse, makes my mouth flutter, like I *want* to say something. Miraculously, the word "hi" manages to squeak its way out.

Sean shifts his weight from side to side in a nervous sort of dance. "Are your parents home?"

I shake my head and look away as he peels off his T-shirt.

"Do you expect 'em soon? I mean, I don't want them to get mad that I'm in your pool or anything."

"They won't be back for a while," I blurt, feeling my heart load up with panic. I take a deep breath to calm myself down, trying to piece together what's really going on here. I mean, there's a good chance that Kelly won't even care. Maybe she won't even find out. And even if she does, I can just say Sean looked like he was gonna pass out from the heat. I guess he sort of does.

"Cool." He twiddles with the strap of his belt for several moments. "I probably shouldn't get these shorts wet." His hand is on the zipper of his long khaki shorts.

I grab the raft for security and begin paddling in a circle. But before I know it, I'm facing him again. A pair of plaid boxer shorts, the cotton kind, I think. A bare chest with that woven stripe of hair right below the navel.

"Just what the doctor ordered," he says, making his way in.

I let out a dorky giggle and begin making waves with the raft.

Sean pushes his feet off the wall of the pool. The blades of his shoulders slice through the skin of the water as he swims across. "This feels incredible," he says. He takes a gulp of water and squirts it out between his teeth like a fan.

It hits my cheek, and I laugh, a bit too hard, making a weird hiccup noise. I consider squirting him back, but that would definitely wash my lipstick off completely.

He disappears under the water and swims around me like a shark. The tiny bits of dirt at the bottom make a spiraling funnel around my ankles. He grabs my calf and yanks me under with him. I feel myself laughing beneath the surface, my mouth and nostrils filling up with water. And then our legs touch and I feel those tiny, prickly hairs that I have studied so intently rub against the skin of my knee and up my thigh, and . . . I freak.

I break the surface of the water and try to catch my breath. I wonder if the touching was a mistake.

Sean comes up and looks at me, and now I'm the one being studied. I grab the raft, squishy from loss of air.

"Nicole?" He places his hand on the raft, a thumblength from mine. It suddenly dawns on me that this is the first time he's said my name. And it sounds so different coming from him, sort of sweet and exotic at the same time.

"Yeah?" I swallow hard, dipping my mouth into the water to hide my lip.

"Did you ever . . . I don't know."

"What?"

"I don't know. It's stupid."

"No, what?"

"I don't know, did you ever, you know, maybe think about you and me?"

"Sean," I say, pushing the raft away, trying to laugh it off as a joke.

"What? *Did* you?"

"I don't know. What kind of question is that? Did *you*?"

He shrugs. "I wouldn't have asked if I didn't."

"Really?"

"Once or twice."

I feel my insides light up like birthday candles, even though this is evil, even though we shouldn't be talking this way. And suddenly I feel sort of . . . free. Like, I know I've known all along, but it suddenly hits me. Kelly isn't here. It's just me. And Sean.

"Maybe," I say.

He edges in closer and I can smell the heat of his breath, like freshly cut grass. "Nicole?" His lips are too close to mine to speak, like they might bump together by forming words. And before I know it, they are kissing mine and I'm feeling this tiny, tingling sensation in my right pinkie. The tingling sparkles through my veins and down my spine and encourages me to kiss him back. I do.

Our legs touch again and I feel myself float toward him. Thighs bumping thighs. Calves weaving through calves.

He covers my lips with his kiss again, and it tastes salty and wet. I press the inside of my knee against his outer thigh and feel the web of bristly hair crawl up my leg.

"Sean," I whisper. I place both palms on the side of the pool and lift my body up to sit on the ledge. "Come on." I take his hand and lead him over to the garden, where it's all pretty and magical, and where no one can see. I look down at his boxers, the button-fly kind, dripping wet, the cotton checks sticking to his . . . *thing*. Sticking out a bit. And I can't look, have to turn away, feel my cheeks get all fiery hot. It suddenly occurs to me that if I wanted to, I could call this whole thing off, tell him that I have to go inside, that I have to go and pick up Maria.

But I don't.

And so I find myself lying on the ground with him, feeling the cool and peppery soil at my back and in the strands of my hair. He rolls himself on top of me, and the wetness of his skin slips against my legs. I slide my hands down his back and glide them up and down his hips, trying to imagine the way Vanessa does it on *Sands of Time*.

Sean moves his hand in between my legs and I think it's the first time he notices my bathing suit has shorts for bottoms—tight, spandex shorts. He rolls us over, sort of on our side, facing one another, and I feel his hand at the back zipper. "Is this cool?" he asks.

I sort of give a nod. It's so easy for him, like he's done this before, like it's no big deal.

I think about Vanessa's first time. How she and Roland had come so close so many times, but then decided to wait. Then, on the anniversary of the day they first met, Roland surprised Vanessa by re-creating a scene from *Night Falls in Star Land*, her favorite storybook. He took her to the planetarium, after hours, because it was winter and too cold outside for a picnic at night. And then they made love right there under the Big Dipper. I think how it was Roland's first time, too.

I feel my shorts being tugged down my hips, but not getting very far. "Can I have some help here?" Sean asks. I lift up my butt and feel the shorts slide down my legs. I kick them from around my ankles with my heels.

And then Sean gets up. He walks over to where his shorts are and scrounges through the pockets. At first he takes his cell phone out, and for a brief but humiliating second I think he's going to make a call, but then he just clicks it off and I get this exciting little jolt up my spine. Like, at least while we're together, he doesn't even care if Kelly calls. He fishes through the other pocket for his wallet, plucks it out, and pulls out a condom.

And I can't believe this is happening. I mean, I've *seen* condoms, have had them thrown at me during various be-safe assemblies at school, but I've never actually held one outside the package. I've heard of girls putting the condom on for the guy, some sort of romantic gesture. I wonder if he'll let me try.

Sitting with his back to me, he throws the torn package into the rose bush and puts it on by himself. I want to see it, to see him—to see what one looks like up close. But his boxers are still on and I can't see anything through their dark green plaid print.

He slides himself back on top of me, pulls his shorts down just far enough, and at first it's all hot and urgent between my legs, and I can't believe I've waited this long to be with him. But then I feel a sharp piece of mulch jam into my right butt cheek. I try to readjust, but then Sean pushes himself inside me—a stinging, ripping, ouching pain. I almost cry out but catch myself before any sound escapes.

I try to relax, to tell myself that this is romantic, in the garden, between the tall and purple irises, the black-eyed Susans, and the pretty rhododendron, that Sean must really like me. I look up into his face, to see his eyes, and what they're thinking. But they're closed, like he's concentrating hard, and his lips are parted with breath.

The phone is ringing inside my house. It's probably Maria, wondering where I am.

I look up into the sky, at the puffy white clouds, and wish it were night or that we were in a planetarium. I wonder if Kelly looks up at the ceiling and thinks these same things. I clench my teeth, wondering when it'll be over, when I'll be able to clean myself up of this dirt and mulch. The phone is still ringing. The machine beeps, but I can't quite make out the voice.

"Nickie," Sean whispers into my ear, followed by a long and laborious moan. And I think how this feels and sounds so different from TV. How nobody but Kelly ever calls me Nickie. How nobody but Kelly ever calls me, period.

Sean rolls off me and pulls his shorts back up, lying on

his back, trying to catch his breath, like he's just run a marathon or something.

He looks over at me and smiles. I smile, too.

Now what? After Vanessa and Roland make love, they usually hug and kiss each other for the rest of the show, tell each other secrets. I rest the tips of my fingers against Sean's dirty cheek and kiss him full on the mouth.

He smiles at me when the kiss breaks and then looks away. "I should probably get going," he says. "I haven't finished with the hedges yet." He wipes a smear of dirt from my forehead and then kisses the spot before getting up to fetch his clothes.

I pull my shorts back up, noticing droplets of blood between my thighs. I wipe them as best I can with my fingers and then stand up, feeling dirt slide between my legs, noticing how sticky I feel, hiding my dirty hands behind my back.

Sean has already dressed. He turns to leave but then stops. And for one relieving moment I think he's going to say something really great. But instead he just smiles, lingers a few moments before turning away.

I watch him leave before washing myself off with the garden hose. A few moments later I hear the lawn mower turn on next door, the sound of the motor revving, like it never even happened—like Sean was never even here. I decide I will clean myself up and then vacuum the dirt out of the pool before going to pick up Maria, so we can prepare for Kelly's welcome-home once and for all.

Maria Krito

SATURDAY, AUGUST 12, 11:45 A.M.

Sadie's about to cut me. She's got the safety pin pressed up to my forearm. Her hands are all jittery, like someone's leaked all the blood out of her veins and shot them up with Pixie Stix sugar. There are smiley faces across her finger-nails, bright pink ones—some with missing eyes where the paint has chipped, others with half chewed–off mouths.

"Hurry up," I say. "If you don't do it, you'll have to go home."

"No!" she whines.

I tear the sign from her T-shirt. This is the second time this week she's come over with a torn piece of notebook paper pinned to her shirt, the words PLEASE DO NOT FEED SADIE handwritten in pretty cursive letters across the page. Must have been a bad week.

"Don't!" she shouts at me.

I laugh at her and crumple the sign up into a paper ball, throw it toward my Tupperware garbage pail. "Your mom's fucked. I'm surprised you don't just tear it off yourself." She looks scared, like I really screwed things up for her. "Hurry up," I say, referring to the pin, trying to take her mind off it.

Her eyes spill over with drippy tears. "Please, Maria, no," she whines.

"Don't act like such a baby. I thought you wanted to be my friend."

"I do." She nods toward the pin, like it will help her.

"Then prove it."

It's been a little goal of mine this past year—to get all my friends to cut me. Not that Sadie's a real friend. She's just a kid who always comes around to bug me. But she *thinks* she's my friend, so that must count for something.

I kick my bare legs back and forth on the bed, my heels bouncing against the naked mattress. I'm thinking about getting a tattoo, one on my arch maybe, but not a butterfly or a snake, or anything lame ass like that. I want a tattoo that no one else has—a squashed chicken with bulging eyes, maybe, or a bunch of rusty nails. When my ex-boyfriend James turned eighteen, he had my face tattooed to his chest, because he said I'd always be in his heart. I laugh whenever I think of him with another girl, with my face coming at her while they're trying to do the nasty.

I look over at Sadie, at how her barrettes, her T-shirt, *and* her open-toe sandals are all Tinker Bell–theme coordinated, like she's five. Even the trim on her white tennis skirt has tiny magic wands floating against the swirly pink fabric.

"How old are you now, anyway?" I ask.

"Eleven," she answers, really concentrating on that pin.

"Well, I'm six years older than you and I don't like hanging out with babies."

If I can get Sadie to cut me, then there'll just be Nicole left. Nicole's the kind of girl who draws smiley faces and happy hearts all over the covers of her notebooks and *still* believes in stuff like happily ever after and making birthday wishes. She's also the only person I know who works at all these different places for free; who participates in walkathon causes, and donates her old stuff to Goodwill and starving children.

I've been trying to get her to cut me for a while now, but every time I ask, she gets all Al-Anon on me; she hugs me extra tight, kisses my cheek, and then doesn't even justify the question with an answer.

Me and Nicole have plans together later. I'm hoping I'll get her to do it then.

I pull a lighter out from the bib pocket of my overalls. "Think your fingernails could be a little dirtier? The least you could have done was wash them. That's so rude." They're all sticky and gross from eating up all my circus peanuts. I grab the safety pin from her grubby fingers and run the point under the flame a few seconds. "Make sure you don't touch me with those. I'll get infected."

I hand Sadie back the pin and she points the tip into my skin. "Worthless," I sing. "Waste of my time."

Her eyebrows stitch together and her mouth forms a tiny frown, her cheeks all extra red and puffy. "No, Maria!" she finally fumes. "I can't. I can't do it." She throws the pin down and turns away from me on the bed.

I'm tempted to lash out at her, to tell her to go home and that I never want to see her again. But I can't. I need to play cool, appeal to her desperate side, use reverse psychology. I say, "That's fine, Sadie. I completely understand. It's not for everybody. I mean, just because all my other friends have done it, doesn't mean that you have to, too. You're just not ready to be my friend, that's all." I stand, head for the door, and open it a crack to let her out.

"No," she whines, pulling at her lashes. "I don't want to leave."

"Will you do it then?"

She shrugs.

I check the clock. It's almost noon. I still have another hour before Nicole is supposed to pick me up. "How about if I take you to Scoops for a double dip. Then will you do it?"

She smiles patty-cake wide, like I just asked her to be my best friend or something.

I peel my wallet open. A buck. One friggin' dollar. That won't even buy us the sprinkles. "Wait here," I tell her.

I peek in on Uncle Luke in the family room. The TV's on, some science show—the mating habits of the mosquito—with crickets chirping in the background. Luke's asleep, his head lolling against the back cushion of the armchair. There's a purple Tupperware tumbler resting in his lap with a stalk of celery sticking out. Bloody Mary, no doubt.

I tiptoe across the rug toward him, doing my best to avoid stepping on the Tupperware orders my mother has scattered across the floor. He keeps his wallet in the front pocket of his pants. I know it's there. The brown wrinkly calf-leather edge is sticking out between his thumb and pointer. I'll have to move his hand to get at it.

Luke churns a bit in his sleep. I scooch down beside him, doing my best to clear away enough room on the floor and be quiet at the same time. His snoring has caused his T-shirt to draw up and expose about an inch and a half of hairy belly. The blub stares me in the face, as does one bright, cherry-red nipple peeping through a dryer-eaten hole. If only his kitchen appliance–buying customers knew what he wears under all that Sears polyester. I reach out for his wrist and he lets out a cartoon-like snore, flops his head to the other side. I have to bite the inside of my cheek to keep from laughing.

I lift his wrist upward and hold it midair, use my other hand to reach into that pocket. And then he grabs me. Throws me across his lap and starts tickling me under the arms. And now it's me who's snorting, wriggling in his grip, trying my best not to piss myself.

"What do you want, huh? What do you want?" he says, jabbing at my sides, snapping my bra. He's such a pig. "Are you looking for some of this?" He pulls his T-shirt back down to cover the blub and takes out his wallet.

"Yeah, I want some of that."

"Well, you know, all you need to do is ask."

Luke stops and I concentrate hard on him, wait to hear what he wants. I watch the way his squinty blue eyes spy at me from behind a pair of tiny, gold-rimmed glasses, the way his lips spout like he's trying to think up what to say, and how his ears are as tiny as mine. I try to imagine what he looked like at my age, before his face got all saggy, and wonder if he might have been kind of cute.

"What do you need the money for?" he asks.

"It's no big deal, Luke. Me and Sadie are just gonna buy ice cream." I curl my tongue so that the barbell pokes out of my mouth. I want to stretch the hole to a size eight or nine, big enough to squirt water through it, right at him.

"Hey, that's Uncle Luke to you." He slides his wallet back into his pocket.

He's not my *real* uncle. My mother's an only child, but that's *still* what she insists I call him. She also insists that Luke's just staying with us for a while. *Staying with us,* not moving in and taking up valuable sofa space for the past *eight* years. My real father was some guy my mother met one night while tending bar at Majors downtown. Apparently, she never saw him again after that night, doesn't even know his name, but she swears she'd recognize that creamy, Swiss-chocolate skin and that perfectly chiseled chin anywhere.

As a result, my skin is chocolate milk—a shade caught somewhere between mocha and latte. A far cry from creamy Swiss chocolate. And an even farther cry from my mother's porcelain white.

She says I sort of look like him, that my chin sort of juts out the way his did and that's where I got my egg-shaped face. She also says I have his dark, nut-brown lips and his even darker mahogany-brown eyes. I'm not sure. I don't know who I look like, or if I even look like anyone.

I just know that my blood is always red.

"Where's your mother?" Luke asks.

"Out. Tupperware meeting." Keeping her status as Diamond Manager requires her to be out a lot.

"Well then, what are you doing later? How about we run down to Movie Mayhem and rent ourselves some Stephen Kings?" Stephen King's my favorite. He knows this.

"What for?"

"Just want to spend some time with my girl."

"Whatever."

"What's that supposed to mean? You used to like to spend time with me."

"Yeah, well, I also used to like to chew aluminum foil, and I don't do that anymore, do I?"

To this, he snaps his fingers back and forth over his head, homegirl style. "What's the mat-ter, Ho-mey?" he raps. *"Chick—chick-chick—chick-ah. Chew-chew-chew.* Don't wanna hang loose with your Uncle Luke? *Chick—chick-chick—chew. Chew-chew-chew.* Spin some disks? Watch some flicks?"

"So cool," I say, interrupting, not able to hide my smile. I make the L-for-Loser sign with my hand and place it up to my forehead.

"You used to think so. Maybe that's just it; maybe you're *too* cool now." He touches my shirt collar to make me look, and when I do, he does that corny finger-glide-up-your-face bit. It's so stupid; I can't help but laugh.

"It's good to see you smile," he says. "For the past couple weeks I've been wondering if you lost your teeth."

Has it been that long?

He keeps me there for a couple minutes, rambling about how I remind him of his (long-lost) daughter, with my rusty voice and tight black corkscrew curls; how he used to take her fishing at some lake, and why don't we go.

And I don't really mind listening to him and his dumb stories, even though I've heard them all before. It kind of makes me feel like I'm somebody else. Like I've been burped out onto the set of some made-for-TV movie, where I'm the typical girl-with-a-problem and he's the overprotective dad. Not Luke the Puke.

"Sadie's waiting for me," I say, looking toward his watch, picturing time melting away like those double dips. "Are you gonna give me the ice cream money or not?"

He shrugs, a stupid grin on his face, like he's having fun, dangling money over my head. "If you do a little something for me," he says finally.

I nod, feel my face fall, saggy like his. Like someone's clicked the channel back to reality TV and I'm Maria all over again.

Back in my room, Sadie's still there. She's sitting on the bed, using up all my blueberry nail polish. "Go outside and hide in the bushes underneath my window. No peeking in."

"Why do I have to go outside?" She's trying to cover up those pathetic little smiles with the blue.

"Because I said so." I position myself in the doorway to show her that I mean business. "Just say good-bye, slam the door, and wait for me there. Then we'll go."

Sadie's bottom lip quivers. "Why?"

"Because you want to go to Scoops. And if you want to go to Scoops, you have to do what I say."

"Why can't I just wait here?"

"I mean it," I insist, ignoring her question. "No peeking. I'll know if you do."

Sadie palms the nail polish and makes her way, slowly but surely, down the hallway, into the kitchen, and out the back door.

The chair in the family room creaks. Luke is getting up.

I leave my bedroom door open a crack—just wide enough so he can see—and then stand in the middle of the room, a stack of dirty ceramic plates at my bare ankles, dinners for one. Facing sort of sideways, not toward the open door, but not away from it either, I unhook the straps of my overalls and flip the bib part down. I recite the Pledge of Allegiance one full time to myself before sliding the overalls down over my hips and past my knees. Stepping out of the pant legs, I pause through the chorus of "Bloody Wand," my favorite Cryptic Slaughter song, playing in my head. Then I kick the overalls and they hit the wall, landing on the heaping stack of Harlequin novels Nicole brought over to Band-Aid me and James's breakup four months ago.

I rub my hands over my hips and thighs, trying my best to smile, to like the way the skin feels. Instead I feel the leftover chicken pock on my upper back thigh. A Hershey Kiss–shaped birthmark on my right hip. I pull my T-shirt up, feel the air greet my gut, a chill wipes over my shoulders as each becomes free. And then it's just me, in my bra and panties.

And I feel nothing.

I toy with the straps of my bra, the frayed fabric at the hem, almost laugh out loud just thinking how old and ratty it is. Then I unhook the back, let my boobs just dangle. I cup them and squeeze them, poke them and tweak them. And when I feel enough is enough, I place my fingers inside the hem of my panties. I shimmy them down in time to Bloody Wand's instrumental part, fighting the urge to play the air guitar. I pick them up with my toe and press them against my cheek, stifle my yawn with the fanny part, all the while trying to act like they're good enough to eat. Yum, yum, yum. Then I slap my ass a few times for my own amusement, have to stop myself from going too fast. Slow, slow, slow. I finger through the black, wiry hair between my legs and imagine fishing line, the days Luke was referring to—him and his daughter at the lake.

Done.

I get dressed quickly, pull a long T-shirt on over my tangerine bikini, in case me and Nicole go back to her house for a swim, poke my arms through the straps of my overalls, and slip into a pair of lime-green flip-flops. I open my bedroom door. There, waiting for me on the dining room table just a few feet away, is Luke's wallet. I open it, take out two twenties, and shove them into my pocket.

Enough money, but not enough time. Nicole will be

here in a half hour. I'll have Sadie cut me and then rain-check her for that ice cream.

I look out my bedroom window. There she is, hiding in the azaleas, just like I told her. She's got her thumb lodged between her strawberry-shaped lips, sucking. "You can come back in," I say, opening the window.

I pull up on the screen so she can climb in. Only, her blub gets in the way and she barely makes it. It takes five full attempts at hoisting herself up before she's finally able to get up on the sill and push her arms all the way through. But then she gets sort of stuck there, midway, her legs sticking straight out the window. I give her a chair to lean on for support. This helps. With some extra pull from me, she makes it.

She takes a seat on the bed, and she's huffing and puff-ing, like climbing through a ground-floor window is any big deal. I hand her the safety pin. She frowns and pulls at her eyelashes.

"Just do it and then we'll go."

She holds the pin up to my arm, but then starts the shaking thing again.

"Do it!" I say, between gritted teeth. "Cut me!"

She scratches me. One long, white slit along my inner forearm, just below the elbow where the skin is dry. Her eyes fill with baby tears. More and more and more. I won-der if she can even see straight.

"Harder," I demand. "You need to press down to break the skin."

ly it's always Kelly jammed in the middle of us, the
between two pieces of bread. Except when I really
her, that is. Nicole is just one of those people who
o help others out, who likes to try and solve every-
problems, including mine.

e's coming over because we're supposed to be plan-
welcome-home party for Kelly, who's been away all
er at her father's in California, but will be home in a
eeks. It was my idea to throw a party. I thought we
go to Celebrations to plan out what to buy, go back
house for a swim, and then somewhere along the
e could finally do it.

wonder if she might be tied up working at the hos-
ome old geezer she delivered flowers to on her shift
have her trapped, chatting about how the good old
e now gone, gone, *gone*.

inger through the individual pins, reminiscing over
ne. My ex-boyfriend James cut me twice. Once on
er back, while we were dating, so he could tag me.
her time it was on my shoulder, just as we were
g up, because he wanted to leave his mark.

en there's Mimi from Dunkies. We used to hang
the time when I worked there two months ago,
ough Kelly always called her a ho-bag. Cutting me
ze her one bit—she had burned a four-inch Celtic
to her own upper arm—so it was really no big deal
er one of us. She didn't so much as blink out of

It takes her a few times to actually make me bleed. And
when she finally does, it's a pretty decent line, about an
inch and a half. It doesn't even hurt, just feels like I
scratched myself on something sharp. I guess I can't expect
too much from a thumb-sucking eleven-year-old.

The blood fills the slit and I wait to see if it'll drip. I
move my arm a bit to guide a trickle, but it just stays put.
I'm tempted to squeeze it, but when I glance up at Sadie,
she looks like she's gonna hurl. She's staring at her finger.
It's got the tiniest bit of blood on it and she's all sick
about it.

"Just wipe it," I tell her.

She does, on my bed, but it doesn't help one bit. Her
mouth is all hangy and her tongue is sticking out over her
teeth. I'll have to wait to squeeze.

Sadie lifts her shirt to blot at her eyes with Tinker
Bell's wings, exposing a roll of fat over her skirt. Like pizza
dough.

I pluck the bloody safety pin from her fingers and lean
across the bed to grab my lunch box. I pull out Sadie's
name tag; I've already written her name across it. The name
tags are really price tags, the tiny square ones with the
string attached where the salespeople tie it to stuff—I man-
aged to collect a bunch of them from the thrift shop before
I quit. I blow a bit on the point, to dry the blood, and then
tie her name tag to the pin.

There's a bunch more like it in my box, safety pins

with their owners' names attached, those who've cut me. I like to carry them around so I always know who my *real* friends are. Not that Sadie will ever be one.

"Now you have to leave," I say. "Nicole will be here any minute."

"What about Scoops?"

"I don't have time. Maybe later. Maybe tomorrow, okay? I promise."

"No," she whines. "Now. You said—"

"Well, now I'm saying *tomorrow*."

"Can't I come with you and Nicole?"

"No."

Sadie folds her arms and stares straight ahead toward my poster of Cryptic Slaughter during their Injurious Harmony tour. She really doesn't want to go home.

"Okay," I cave. "You can stay. But I'm padlocking the door so you can't leave my room unless it's through the window, and you can't make any noise, and you can't use any of my stuff. Got it?"

She nods.

I've let her stay here before when I've gone out; with the door locked, she's safe. It's not like anyone here notices anyway. Plus, I feel bad sending her home—somehow, her house seems even more screwed up than mine.

Sadie takes her Game Boy out of her skirt pocket and camps out on the beanbag chair in the corner.

"You still have that old thing?" I ask her.

Sadie shrugs, whining something [...] sister's, how her mother won't buy [...] game stuff. Meanwhile, I grab my lun[...] all the pins, all my cuts. Eleven of the[...] couple were done by the same person[...]

I've written all of my friends' [...] names of people I don't hang arou[...] Slowly, each of these tags gets attached[...] She finally cut me after I lied and said [...] was spreading rumors about her—tha[...] a bad one at that. Personally, I don't [...] cares what he thinks. Who'd want to [...] mother fixed them up with anyway? [...] exchange for the information—for so[...] I made up. I guess everybody has a pr[...]

I wonder where I'll have Nicole [...] and most of this morning I've psych[...] ing how today she'll finally do it. I g[...] mother's Tony Robbins tapes is maki[...] have whatever I want. Like everyone e[...] Nicole has to give, and when she final[...] cut to my inner thigh, or my belly, or [...] Though it seems easier for people to d[...] that makes a difference, like my arm [...] rest of me.

It's a little after one o'clock. I won[...] It's kind of weird to be going out, [...]

Usua[...] fillin[...] need[...] likes[...] bod[...]

ning[...] sum[...] few [...] cou[...] to l[...] line[...]

pita[...] mig[...] day[...]

eac[...] my [...] Th[...] bre[...]

ou[...] ev[...] di[...] kn[...] fo[...]

42   43

sequence when I told her I wanted it on my chest, right over my heart. She just did it. Sort of a waste of a pin.

Jessie, the papergirl, was one of the first people to cut me. It was almost a year ago. She used to try and throw the rolled-up *Salem News* toward our front steps to avoid coming up to the door. On collection day, though, she had no choice.

"Is it that time already?" I asked as I opened the door. She just nodded and looked down at her moccasins. "Now, let me see here." I reached deep into my Levi's, pretending to scrounge for a couple bucks. "I don't think I have any money. Do *you* have any?"

She didn't answer, just kept looking down at those ridiculous beads, threaded together at the toe of her shoe in the form of an orange Indian with blue jeans.

"You're scared of me, aren't you, Jessie?"

She shook her head.

"I don't want you to be scared of me. I just want to be your friend. Do you want that, too?"

She shook her head again, mouthed a tiny no.

"That's sad, you know that? That really hurts my feelings."

She shrugged.

"So, what *do* you want?" I asked.

"I want you to leave me alone."

"Fair enough. I'll leave you alone. But you have to do something for me first." She finally looked up at me as I pulled the safety pin out of my pocket. "I want you to cut me. Right here." I pointed toward my forearm.

"*What?*" she cracked out—the loudest I'd ever heard her voice. "What's *wrong* with you?"

"It's not going to kill me or anything. I'm just doing this experiment."

She crinkled her eyebrows together and made a sour face. "You're crazy!"

To that, I grabbed at the front of her pants and pried the roll of ones and fives from her pocket. "I bet you want to cut me now."

"Give it back, Maria. I'll have you arrested."

"And I'll make your life hell." I held the safety pin out to her.

She hesitated, then took it. "Just an experiment?" she asked.

"Exactly."

She held the point up to my flesh and scratched like a cat. "There."

"No," I said. "The rule is, you have to make me bleed."

She didn't do it right then. It took more than five full months of psyching her out, glaring at her in gym class, and throwing her impossible-to-read smiles—sometimes evil, sometimes delirious, mostly sheer cunning—as I passed her in the hallway.

And so began my mission, making sure I was home on collection day, making sure *I* was the one to answer the door, to harass her, to try and make deals with her, to take her money.

When she finally did go through with it, I kept my promise and never so much as blinked in her direction again. I kind of regretted making that promise, though. I wonder what it would be like to have a friend like Jessie, if it'd be anything like having an extra Nicole around when you need one.

I look at the clock. It's one thirty. Where the hell *is* Nicole? Sadie peeks up at me from her Game Boy, like she's enjoying that Nicole isn't here yet. I guess I'll give her a call.

The phone rings and rings, but then it's the answering machine that picks up. She's probably on her way, probably just running late. I hang up and glance over at my lunch box. There's a name tag sticking out. Nicole's. I try her number again. "Hi, Nicole," I say, after the beep. "It's me, Maria. I'm not even sure what time it is, but I didn't know if we'd be going swimming after we went to the mall, and if I should have my bathing suit. . . . You're probably on your way now anyway, so I guess I'll just bring it in case. I've spent all day planning out Kelly's party and can't wait for you to hear my ideas. Okay, I guess I'll see you soon. Bye."

I hang up. Leaving the message makes me feel better, like maybe she just fell asleep, and between the phone ringing and my voice on the machine, has gotten up and will be calling me back any minute to say she'll be right over.

I decide that when she does call, I'll need to have that list of party ideas ready. I open up an old chem notebook and start brainstorming on the blank pages in the back.

PLACE: Nicole's house = pool.
SURPRISE TACTIC: Nicole invites Kelly
for swim. Kelly comes around to backyard—
we'll all be there.
DATE: ??? Discuss with Nicole.
WHO'LL BE INVITED: Me, Nicole, Sean,
Emily, Matt, Kory, ?
THEME: Something tropical? A luau?
FOOD: Pizza—good because cheap.
Pineapple chunks on the pizza? Funky
green punch served in gutted pineapples.
FAVORS: Grass skirts, Hawaiian leis.

I'm actually excited now about the party, about telling Nicole all my ideas. I look at the clock. It's five minutes before two. What the fuck? Why is Nicole doing this? Why hasn't she even called?

I turn my back to Sadie and squeeze my arm hard so that the blood oozes through the freshly crusted slit, like ketchup through used-up packets. I touch the blood, get it on my fingertips, wonder if I've bled at least a teaspoon altogether. I squeeze again, waiting for the blood to seep out just a little more. But when it doesn't, I pick up the phone again.

"Hi, Nicole. It's me again. Are you home? It's two o'clock and I don't know where you are. You were supposed to pick me up. If you're in the shower, give me a call when you get out. I really need to see you. I really need to talk."

I click the receiver off. I don't know what I'll tell her when she asks why I need to see her so bad or what I need to talk about. Usually all I have to do is give the slightest hint that I'm not doing well, and there she is on my doorstep with IOU tickets to Cryptic Slaughter, copies of her favorite books, or a wad of tissues to cry into.

Unlike Kelly. Not that Kelly isn't a good friend. We have good times together, she and I. It's just been different ever since she cut me. Nicole has sort of been the only constant in my life; the only one I've ever relied on. Even though she hasn't cut me yet.

There's a knock on my bedroom door.

Luke.

"Maria?" he calls, his head turned sideways, his spouty lips just visible through the door crack.

"Yeah?"

"Did you want to go down to the video store? Get those movies?"

My skin ices over. "I don't know. I might be going out."

"Well, let me know, okay?"

"Yup."

I pick up the phone, try Nicole's number again. This time it's busy. A warming relief. I try again. The machine. "Nicole? Are you there? It's me, Maria. If you're home, pick up. I need to talk to you. Please . . . it's important. We're supposed to go out today. Where are you?"

I wait. And wait. And then the machine disconnects me.

I can hear Luke pacing in the kitchen, his wingtipped shoes against the cold ceramic tiles. I try Nicole again. This time it just rings and rings.

No machine. No Nicole. No nothing.

"You have to leave," I tell Sadie.

"Why?" she asks, her eyes and thumbs still glued on the Game Boy. "If she's not coming, why can't we just do something?"

"Go!" I choke out. I can feel my chest get tight, like someone's tying it up in strings. Can feel my eyes fill up with tears.

"Just another minute," Sadie says, probably finishing up a level.

"NO! NOW!"

I think I've scared Sadie shitless. She pops the Game Boy back into her pocket, wrestles up from the beanbag chair, and walks toward the door without another look in my direction—a firm finger-clamp to the eyelashes; lips,

50

rosebud tight; and cheeks, red like fireballs.

When she leaves I tear the list of party ideas from my notebook and rip it up into a hundred tiny meaningless pieces. I open up my lunch box and take out a safety pin. I hold it between my teeth so I can take down the straps of my overalls, pull up on my T-shirt.

And free up my belly.

I rub my palm across the fuzzy tan skin. With the other hand I'm able to unhook the needle part from its fastener. I stare at the point. Then push it into the left side of my belly. Down, as far as I can bear to make it go. It stings so sharp; I almost have to close my eyes. But I can't. I want to watch. I want to see everything.

With gritted teeth and watery eyes, I glide the pin across my stomach, past my belly button, and to the other side. One long clean slit. The blood fills the crack and bubbles up at the seam. I have to pinch the flesh hard to get the blood to trickle down, toward my lap, in quick tiny teardrops.

I sit there on the floor, squeezing, blotting, and re-squeezing, for as long as my belly will let me. Then I rip Nicole's name tag up and toss the paper bits to the floor. Since she was never my real friend anyway.

Kelly Pickerel

It was the way he talked about her. The way his eyes
filled up, like the tears could drown you in just one blink.
The way his dimpled chin trembled when he spoke. How
his voice was all splintery, slivered into a million pieces—
all about her, about how much he loved her and couldn't
accept that this had happened, that he had done it.

The trial had lasted a little over two weeks. But I
watched it a lot longer than that. Thanks to Court TV and
my VCR, I watched every night before I went to bed and
sometimes until the sky turned blue again. Some nights I

just couldn't say good-bye, couldn't bring myself to look into those watery eyes or hear that broken voice and shut the power off. That would be like abandoning him in some way—leaving him all alone in that cold, impersonal courtroom, trapped in the TV.

I'd play and replay the tape, noticing new things each time. Like that his hair was really dark, dark brown, rather than black like all the papers said. And that he had a Madonna-like mole on his bottom lip that moved with his mouth when he talked.

The tape became fuzzy in parts. Parts where it was his turn to talk about Melanie. When he said how nothing else meant anything, including prison, or death, or whatever else they might do to him, if he couldn't see her every day, if she couldn't read him one of her poems.

I just never knew someone could love that much.

I look over at the armchair in the corner of my room. My clothes are already laid out. My yellow sundress—the short flowy one I'm wearing in the photo I sent him; the barbell necklace Maria made me when her tongue hole stretched and she upgraded to a size six (not the classiest piece of jewelry, but she said it was for luck and it looks kind of cool); my strappy black sandals with the two-inch heels (so I'll be tall enough to talk to him and not feel like I'm five). The same heels that have the straps that cut into my skin and make blisters—a necessary sacrifice.

And my new silky pink bra. I unravel it from the

pink-and-white-striped paper the saleslady wrapped it in, and hold it up to my chest. They're demi-cups, with scalloped pink sheering that borders the top, and a tiny plastic clasp in between. I hope it's the kind he meant.

I wore a bra kind of like this on my date with Derik LaPointe last year. Derik was this guy my mother fixed me up with, the son of some friend of hers. And while I never meant for him to see it, I kind of knew he would. And then he did.

My date with Robby will be different.

I manage to get the dress on, despite my fumbling fingers at the back zipper, make my way over to the mirror, and take a peek. And suddenly—even though I've come this far, or maybe *because* I've come this far—I feel sick. Like I can't possibly go through with it.

I yank the hot rollers from my hair and flop back onto the bed, pull the covers up to my middle. I think back to how this whole thing started, with just one innocent letter.

But then there were more letters. Five and a half years' worth. Five and a half years of him constantly asking me for my phone number. Me, forever ignoring the question. Both of us feeding into each other's idea of fantasy and sharing our deepest secrets—how we'd meet when he got out; all of our plans for when and where; how my father lives in Santa Cruz, and isn't that so close?

And I never really intended any of it. Mostly.

March 5, 2001

Dear Robby:

I almost can't believe I'm writing this (no offense). I mean, I've just never written to someone famous before. Do you think of yourself as famous? I guess it must be pretty weird knowing that you're on TV every day, that practically all of America is watching you. That's pretty much why I'm writing. I watched the trial and I just want to let you know that I'm on your side. I know in the deepest place in my heart that you didn't mean to do it. I could tell. I knew it the moment you parted your lips to speak about Melanie, how much you loved her, how you couldn't imagine living without her, and now you have to. Your voice got all crackley (sp?) and your eyes were like tiny black rocks, washed up on the beach, all wet from the ocean's tears.

The truth is, I've never been in love. But when I am, I hope he loves me as much as you loved Melanie, and I hope I'm smart enough to know what I have. I can't imagine loving someone so much and having them never want to see me again.

Anyway, I guess I just wanted you to know that I don't think you're a monster like some people are saying. In case you're wondering about me, I'm fifteen years old and a sophomore at Salem High School in Massachusetts. I love poetry but I hate gym. You can write to me if you want, and I'll write back.

Yours truly,

Kelly Pickerel

———✕✕✕———

Dear Robby:

Thanks for writing me back!! To answer your questions, I love going to the movies and I also love shopping. My favorite food is pizza. No, I don't have a boyfriend. And NO, I absolutely hate school!!! You are the first person I've ever heard of that misses it. You must be really smart to skip a grade and have to take all honors classes. The only class I like is English, because we get to write poems. Computers isn't bad either. My teacher, Mr. Vargas, is soooo nice!

So what do you do all day in prison? What's it like? What's suicide watch? Are all the inmates on it? Feel free to tell me whatever you want. I'm here for you.

Oh, and sure, I can send you a picture, but it'll have to wait until I can get a current one. I just have old, dorky school pictures. If it helps, I have long blond hair and blue eyes. I'm five-six and my friends say I'm pretty. That's about it. Write Back Soon!!!!

Kelly

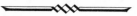

April 20, 2002

Dear Robby:

Your last letter really made me think. I mean, I guess I really am lucky. I'd be totally bummed if I lost all my friends over something that was beyond my control. I mean, it WASN'T YOUR FAULT. It was an accident, a crime of passion. Why can't people see that?!?

Anyway, yes, I guess I do have a lot of friends. Well, two main ones, Nicole and Maria, and they couldn't be more different from each other. And no, I don't tell them EVERYTHING, the way some girls do. I know what you mean—people who just blab about everything and then spread rumors. I like to keep some things secret, too. I guess I just never really thought about it before.

I REALLY like having you as a friend. I've never really had boys as friends before and it's kind of cool. You get me thinking about lots of different stuff. Do you like having me as a friend, too? I hope you do. Sometimes when I get upset about something, I go up in my room and close my eyes and remind myself that you're out there writing me letters. When you get out of prison, you should come to Mass. You can meet all my friends—forget your old fair-weather ones!!!

Hey, I'm including some yummies with this letter—say good-bye to the stale Fig Newtons they're feeding you. Hope you like chocolate. I'm giving you my favorite ones—Snickers, Mr. Goodbars, and Milky Ways. Let me know if you have any special requests of your own and I'll see what I can do!!!

Your TRUE friend,
Kelly

———————◇◇◇———————

October 10, 2003

Dear Robby:

I'm glad you're not mad at me for lying about my age. But that's why I can't give you my phone number. My mom thinks fourteen is too young to talk to boys on the phone, which is SO RETARDED!!! The whole reason I lied was because I didn't want you to think I was too young to write to. As you can see from my pictures, I look older than my age, so I guess I've always just thought of myself as older. Anyway, I'm only three and a half years younger than you, and when you get out at twenty-one, I'll already be seventeen!!!

Anyway, you asked me if I've had a lot of boyfriends, and the answer is no. I wish you could move here and be my boyfriend. I'll never understand why Melanie wanted to break up with you. You loved her SO much! Any girl would be psyched to have someone like you love them.

I'm glad you feel like you can tell me anything. You can. It doesn't freak me out. You can even talk more about that day if you want to, or more about your nightmares. Anything. Don't worry, you won't scare me. I won't leave you.

By the way, I think it's so romantic that when you open my letters you always try to put your mouth on the envelope seal because my mouth has been there, like a special kiss. I can picture your mouth doing it. I'll do the same from now on.

Luv ya,
Kelly

P.S. Glad to hear you're working out every day, you need to be strong to protect yourself in there.

P.P.S. Here's a poem I wrote for you:

Apart

Don't quite know how our pieces fit
But we're part of the same, that's how our candle
     stays lit.
Sometimes I feel like my life has a hole.
And then I hear from you and I'm ready to roll.
You're locked inside and I don't have the key.
I'm in the dark, anything but free.
Apart we are. And apart we'll be.
And until we're together, there won't be a
     full me.

<hr>

November 26, 2005

Dear Robby:
   DON'T WORRY!!! You shouldn't be so worried about
other guys. I only told you about that Sean-guy thing
because I was mad at Nicole and I know I can tell you
anything. So here's the way it happened, EXACTLY.
Nicole likes Sean. She tries to flirt with him, but he just
doesn't get it, and she refuses to ask him out. So, for
the longest time, she was trying to get _me_ to get
him _for_ her. She even had me call his house and ask

him if he wanted to go to a dance with her—soooo embarrassing! Anyway, I started talking to him during class, seeing if he had a girlfriend, if maybe he wanted one. But then he started liking me, and now he wants to go out with me. Ugh!!!

Enough of that, what I really want to tell you is that I think about you all the time. I even went shopping last night and bought stuff I thought you would like. A pair of clunky black pumps, this plaid schoolgirl miniskirt with navy blue kneesocks, and a short baby tee that shows off my tummy.

Then, the other day on my way home from school, I walked through this park near my house and stopped a sec. It was weird. I had this amazing feeling that you were there somewhere. With me. Watching me. So I guess I was kind of looking for you, studying all the faces walking by. Were you there? Don't answer that. I want to think that you were. Because soon you will be. I can't believe you'll be out in nine months! How about I visit my father in Cali this summer, so I can see you.

I think it's so romantic that when you get one of my letters, you try to imagine me breathing my words into your ear. And it's so romantic that you smell every one, trying to get a whiff of my shampoo or the inside of my bedroom. I'm spraying this letter with some of my new perfume. It's called *A Minuit*, which means "at midnight." I thought it might be cool if next Tuesday night, at midnight (that should give you enough time to receive this), you could take out my letter, along with the picture of me I sent you, the one where my hair's down and I'm wearing the yellow sundress. I thought maybe you could smell the letter and think of me. I'll do the same (think about you). I'll even wear the yellow sundress. And it will be like we're both together, me right beside you, my warm breath whispering in your ear. Lame? Probably, but just humor me. Okay?

> Until our date on Tuesday,
> Kelly

P.S. I love you too.

P.P.S. Just to give you a mental image of me right now. It's nighttime and everyone's asleep but me. I just got out of the bath, so my hair's all wet. I'm in my room, lying on my bed, wearing a Lakers T-shirt that goes down to my knees, Baby Soft bath cologne, and nothing else.

It's almost ten. A lump forms in my chest. I swallow to try and dissolve it, but it feels like it's only getting bigger.

What if I'm not what he expects? Or . . . what if I'm exactly what he expects? I know he says he loves me, but will he love me in person? And could he possibly love me as much as Melanie?

I move over to the dresser and take out the last ingredient of my outfit, the last stitch I've promised to wear.

Even more important than the bra, the panties are pink and silk and two sizes too small. They're the bikini kind that dip low in the front and have accordion-like straps on the sides. I wouldn't normally buy a pair like this, especially because they cost nineteen dollars and give me permanent wedge, but they're the kind he wanted. I just hope the color's right—that the pink is pale enough, but not too light. That he doesn't tear them the way Derik did.

I haven't told anyone about Robby, even though sometimes it's practically killed me. Like when I came up with the idea for our Tuesday night smell-my-perfume-and-we'll-think-of-each-other date. I *so* wanted to tell Nicole. It just seemed like the romantic kind of thing she'd have thought up. Or when I needed advice about whether or not I should even come to California.

But keeping him a secret, all mine, where no one else can touch or ruin him for me, makes it better. More romantic.

Plus, I can just imagine what Nicole would say about me pen-paling with a convicted murderer. She just wouldn't understand. *No one* would understand. I even say the words aloud to myself sometimes, only to find that it sounds different in the air, out my mouth, so far from my heart.

I unpin the price tag and slip the panties on. The seams cut into my cheeks and thighs, as do the accordion straps at my hips. I wonder if maybe Melanie might have had a pair just like them; if she was ever scared of Robby, or just drawn to his excitement. Or maybe it was a little of both.

I try to imagine what she was thinking that day, her fifteenth birthday, just after the family party, when he suggested they take a walk up that dirt path behind the school to talk. If she played the whole breakup speech over in her head before she actually said it.

If she even saw the rock coming.

Standing at the mirror, I try to concentrate on my face, on putting on my makeup. My lipstick—Fuzzy Peach #9. But there are other faces I can't seem to blot out of my mind. Faces of the jury when the lawyers showed the rock, still stained with Melanie's blood. When the pictures of her head were flipped in front of them. This one woman, sitting to the right. Her cheeks, bubbling up and then exploding into a thousand puffs, like she couldn't breathe, like she was going to pass out.

There are hives dotted across my chest like navigational points. I need to breathe, to relax. Robby would never hurt me. He served his time. He paid for his mistakes. Plus, it was an accident. I've thought so all along. An *accident*. I remind myself of these things all the way down the stairs and into the kitchen for breakfast. Only, I can't possibly eat.

Grace, my father's wife (though, young enough to be my older sister) is hunched over her usual dry toast with black coffee, and doing today's crossword puzzle. "Where's Dad?" I ask.

No answer.

"Hello?"

"Oh, hi," she says, finally noticing me. "There's coffee and muffins on the counter."

"Not hungry."

She eyes me up and down, from my chlorine-yellow hair—a victim of my father's pool—to my French-manicured toes, and then nods. Whatever that means. Tina and Chelsea, my four-year-old half sisters, chase each other into the kitchen and hop into the booth seat, opposite Grace.

"Are you coming to the zoo with us, Kelly?" Chelsea asks.

I look at Grace. Her face is blank, like I could scribble all over it (and wouldn't I like to). The lump in my chest breaks, and shards splinter into my gut. I don't know why it bothers me, why I let it, or why I even care.

"Oh, yeah," Grace says, in her deadpan tone. "Your father and I are taking the twins to the zoo today. Of course you're welcome to join us."

"Kelly's coming! Kelly's coming!" Tina shouts.

Grace looks at Tina, wishing, I suspect, that she had a muzzle handy.

"I have plans," I say, turning on my heel, making my way across the marble-tiled floor, hearing Grace ask the twins for a three-letter word for *angry*.

I find my father in his office, doing the kind of take-home work my mother used to complain about. "I'm going out," I announce to him.

"That's fine," he says. "Give us a call if you need a ride home."

"I'll probably just have Robby drop me off."

"Okay, Kell, have a good time."

I feel like blurting out that it's Robby Mardonia. Robby I-killed-my-girlfriend-because-she-tried-to-break-up-with-me Mardonia. But I don't even think it would matter. So why does it matter to me?

I go back upstairs to spritz on a healthy amount of *À Minuit*. I wonder if Robby can still smell it on my letters. I picture him curled up beside them on some roll-away cot, thinking about the two of us.

I probably should have told him more about Sean, told him that we *did* end up dating after all. Part of me dated Sean out of spite. After I told Nicole he wanted to go out with me, she said we'd have nothing in common. When I asked her what she meant, she shrugged and said that one of us would probably get bored. I didn't need to guess who she meant.

But it wasn't just spite. Part of me wanted to go out with Sean because he was sweet and nice and simple. And did his homework. And volunteered on the yearbook staff. And because Nicole, one of the people I trust most in this world, trusted him.

Then there was the simple truth—Sean was nothing like Derik LaPointe. All fingers and hands. So when Nicole confirmed the fact that she was *over* Sean, that she wanted to forget about him, it pretty much sealed the deal for me. And Sean and I ended up a couple. And, I'll have to admit, it's been sort of nice.

I suddenly feel guilty. I look down at my watch. It's a little after one o'clock on the East Coast, which means Sean's probably just finishing up his landscaping job. I still have a few extra minutes. Maybe I should call him. Maybe the sound of his voice will thwack me to my senses, make me realize that this is completely insane.

Or maybe I'll just want to see Robby all the more.

I pick up the phone and dial. It goes straight to voice mail.

I take it as a sign, hang up, squeeze into the blister-making sandals, and head out to meet Robby.

We're meeting at the diner in Robby's hometown. I know exactly where it is. I made it one of my first must-sees when I got here. It was weird being inside the place after Robby had talked so much about it, after picturing him in there, amid the red-and-white-checked tablecloths, the shiny black vinyl booths and the bright aqua jukebox in the corner, loaded with tunes by Elvis and the Beatles.

When I get off the bus, I can see the diner in the near distance, two blocks away. I look down at my watch. It's after ten thirty. Robby's probably already inside. I hurry down the street, feeling the sandal straps bite into the backs of my heels.

The bells on the diner door jangle as I push it open. I look around. There are several couples seated in booths. One woman and her daughter at the jukebox. An older man talking to the waitress. And two stray males at each end of the counter. Both look up when I enter. One is dressed in army fatigues. He has military-short, jet-black hair, with a five-o'-clock-shadowy chin, and just enough pump in his arms—not too bulky. I'm thinking it's him, thinking he must be about twenty-one. He sort of smiles at me as he takes a sip of coffee. I smile back.

But it's the other guy that stands up, allows his napkin to roll right off his lap. "Kelly," he says.

"Yeah?" I feel myself cringe inside. I feel like, for one horrible-bitchy-mean little moment, I should deny who I am and go flying out the door.

His hair is parted to the extreme left side, dad-style, and he's wearing plumber-loose jeans that hang around his hips. Where Army-guy's arms are perfectly bulgy, Robby's are overly rounded from too much prison food. What happened to all the working out he was supposedly doing? I feel hopelessly shallow sizing him up this way. *The guy has been in prison, for God's sake.*

"Hi," I say finally, noticing that the jeans are brand new, still dark, dark blue, not yet baptized from the wash. His dress shirt, as well, is still in creases from the package.

He smiles at me, then laughs. And we both kind of stand there, me at the door and him in the corner, not really knowing what to do.

The longer I stare, the more I can tell that it's him. Same green-blue eyes. Same slender nose. That heart-shaped chin. Just older. And maybe more average.

Still, it's him, and I can't believe it. I can't believe this is real.

He starts to walk toward me, and he can't stop smiling, like there's a giant boomerang wedged in his mouth.

"Robby?" I say.

"Finally," he says. "It's so good to see you, to hear your voice."

Before I can reply, he slips me into his arms and wraps me up like a pretty package. I touch the tip of my nose to the lobe of his ear and breathe for him—into his ear, the way he likes, and he smells like Ivory soap tangled in spearmint gum. Not quite the salty scent of virility I'd imagined. He holds me there, like this is normal, in a diner, in front of everyone. Like nothing else matters, and maybe nothing else does. "You look perfect," he whispers.

When we finally break, he motions for us to take a seat

in one of the booths. "Thanks for coming all this way," he says, sliding in across from me.

"Sure," I say, trying to free my heels of their straps. "It was no big deal." But he's barely even listening. He's just . . . staring. "Are you hungry?" I grab the menu.

"Are you nervous?" he asks.

My first reaction is to lie, but he knows me too well. Knows just about everything, things I barely even tell myself. "Yes."

"Well, don't be. It's just me, remember?" He takes my hand and draws a figure eight in the palm, over and over and over again. "I'm nervous, too," he admits. "What are *you* nervous about?"

"I don't know. I guess I'm scared of what you might think of me." That *was* the way I'd been feeling, for the past five and a half years, but now, at this instant, I'm not sure if I even care. I readjust myself in the seat, trying to free my crack from the silk wedge.

"You don't know?" He stops drawing in my palm, mid figure eight.

I peek up at him. At those eyes, so Melanie-serious, like he has no doubts.

"I'm not one to judge you, Kelly. I love you."

He loves me. It sounds so strange hearing him say it. So weird that I have to bite back the jolt I feel stretch across my face. But then I have to remind myself that I told him the same. In so many letters, I told him *I* loved *him*.

But this person sitting in front of me isn't the person I wanted. The person I want is the one I can run back home to, the one I can write a letter to, describing this horrible confusion in my head.

He's staring at me so hard; I don't even think he cares if I say it back. I decide to be honest. I say, "This is just so weird. I mean, we've been writing back and forth for so long. I guess I'm not quite sure what we're supposed to do."

I think about my pink bra and panties and feel stupid even talking. I take the cell phone out of my bag and rest it on the seat beside me, just in case Sean calls.

"We're supposed to be together." He beams. "Finally. Are you as happy as I am?"

I nod and look down at the menu to take a break from what I'm feeling. "Are you hungry?"

"Sure, we should eat something," he says.

As I study the menu, he points out items I might be interested in—things he knows I like to eat. Cheese omelet, peanut-butter pancakes, strawberry blintzes. And, it's like, for some reason, I don't want him to know these things about me. I don't want him to know me at all.

We order, and the waitress, this freckly, red-haired girl, brings us some coffee.

"How are things at your dad's?" he asks. "How's Grace?"

"Fine," I say, trying to take my eyes off the pen in his

front shirt pocket. What was he thinking by putting a pen in there? Why does he even need one? "I might be going to the zoo with them later."

"Oh?" He swishes the spoon back and forth in his coffee mug, stirring over the disappointment that hangs on his face. "I thought we had plans."

I want to grab the menu back, to escape this conversation. But after several seconds of awkward silence, he changes the subject and starts talking about the motel he's staying in and how he wants to get a job painting houses so he can go to school. And all the while he's talking, I can't help but think—is this the same guy who spoke that way on the stand about Melanie? The one who told me the most beautifully intimate secrets in his letters? Who made me a poet?

He stops talking and looks at me for a response. I have no idea what the question is. "Yeah," I say, hoping *yeah* is the appropriate answer.

"Have you listened to a word I've said?"

"Yes." A tweak of snappiness in my voice. "Your motel is cramped and you want to study law enforcement."

"Criminal law," he corrects. "What's wrong? Do you still feel guilty about telling your mother you wanted to spend the summer with your dad?"

And I hate it. That he knows these pieces of me.

That he knows I lied to my mother about coming here. That a couple of weeks before I came, I cut Maria on the arm with a safety pin because she begged me to do it. But more because she wouldn't tell me what Derik LaPointe was saying about me behind my back until I made at least one slit. I told Robby how guilty I felt about it afterward, especially when I saw Maria tear up. How nothing Derik LaPointe could possibly say about me could compare to the look on her face.

"Yeah, I guess that's it."

"You need to forgive yourself. If there's one thing I've learned in this life, it's that forgiveness starts with the self."

I almost want to cover my ears. I don't want to hear his Oprah-friendly advice. And I especially don't want my mistakes—stuff no one's supposed to know about me—thrown up in my face. But he knows all my faults. Every one.

I think about how I told him all about my date with Derik LaPointe. How we had taken a walk through the park after this party and what we did there. How I let him. Because I knew how much my mother wanted me to go out with a "nice boy" like him. Because she never thinks I do anything right.

"Is there something wrong?" he asks.

I ignore the question and lean back, allowing the waitress to smack a ceramic plate full of peanut-butter pancakes in front of me.

I think about when I told him how ugly I feel all the time. How I'd give anything to have a dryer-sheet life like Nicole's—clean, stark, habitual.

I even told him about the times I've wanted to make it all stop.

"I'm not hungry," I say finally.

"What's wrong?" he asks.

"I don't know." I push my plate away. "This is just a little too real for me."

"What are you talking about? We've waited almost six years for this. I love you. I thought you said you loved me, too."

"I did."

"*Did?* Or *do?*"

"I'm sorry, Robby." I feel myself get up, and I almost can't believe I'm actually leaving. Like this. It's horrible, and I feel every bit of it, like my heart is slowly hollowing itself out.

But I need to get away. This isn't the way I wanted it.

The door bells jangle behind me as I leave. I manage a few steps before freeing the straps from the backs of my heels, the skin all mangled and watery, blood outlining the place where the blisters have popped. I almost expect him to come running after me, to ask me to take a walk down some long dirt path. But I guess he doesn't love me as much as he thinks, as much as he loved Melanie.

SATURDAY, AUGUST 12, 2:45 P.M.

So I'm just starting my shift at Red's, and in she walks. Just like that. Just after seeing her at the video store, like, twenty minutes ago. She even takes a seat at my station. Like after all this time of bumping into each other but not really saying anything, we're finally going to meet. And I think, this time I'm definitely going to talk to her.

The first time I saw her was at the beginning of last year. It was at this party I went to with a girl my parents asked me to take out—this girl Kelly from school, the daughter of some friends of theirs. I didn't talk to her then, *because* I was with Kelly, *and* because she wasn't the kind of girl I normally went for. Not that she's butt or anything. She's cute. *Really* cute. Long black hair tucked behind her ears. Hula-girl hips, and a pretty fine rack. Darkish skin and huge, light brown eyes. She looks like she's Asian or Hawaiian or something, like a foreign-exchange chick from some tropical island.

She saw me, too. I know she did. We sort of played eye-tag all night, but she saw I was with that Kelly chick. And she was with some guy, too, some short guy with dreads, some guy who obviously didn't know that dreads went out with raver jeans.

I saw her a few more times after that. Once at the newsstand when I was with Debbie, this skank I was seeing. She walked right by us, smiled at me, picked up a package of bubble gum cigarettes, smiled again, bought it, and left.

About a month later, it was at Starbucks. She was sitting in the corner, reading some book. I was about to go up and talk to her, but then it was my turn in line, and the guy behind the counter had been trying to get my attention, and there were all these people behind me getting pissed off because I had my head up my ass, gawking at some girl. Then she looked up and saw that I was just staring at her, like a pervert or something, getting all these people pissed, and so I tried to act cool, like they were the ones with the problem, and ordered a large Coolatta. *A fucking large Coolatta at a Starbucks.* The guy at the counter told me I was in the wrong place, and so I agreed, like I was lost or something, and left. I just left—my fucking tail caught between my fucking legs.

Today I'm not leaving. And neither is she. Not until we actually speak to each other.

She's sitting at the counter, her hair up in one of those bunlike things, with these long wooden sticks puncturing the center from both sides. And she's got this huge pocket-book. It's made up of all these different colored strings and fabrics, like she put it together herself with stuff she had lying around the house. I wonder what she has in there, why she needs a bag that big. She unzips it, takes out a pair of glasses—black rectangular ones. She puts them on and picks up the menu.

"You've got someone at Eight," my mother yells out to me.

No shit I've got someone at Eight. I realize I'm just standing here, resting my ass against the cash register drawer, chain-eating the fries off somebody's dirty plate, almost forgetting the fact that, since she's at my station, I actually have to go up and talk to her.

Seeing her today at Movie Mayhem would have been the perfect time to say something to her. I almost did; I had the line I was going to use down and everything. I was gonna say, "What's the one film you can name that has altered your way of thinking most profoundly?" Total snatch material. But then this old guy intercepted me to try and get in her pants.

I couldn't believe his routine. He kept asking her all these questions about movies he'd pick up off the rack, if she thought his niece would like them. Like she'd freakin' know. She tried to ignore him for the most part, but that didn't seem to shake him, and then I hear her ask, "Well, what kind of movies does your niece like?" And he says, "She really likes Stephen Kings." So she says, "Why not check out the Horror section?" And then he just sits there and stares at her for, like, half a minute and says, "Because *you're* checking out the New Releases." Total freakin' perv. So then I hear him ask her if she'd like to come join them at *his* place for the King marathon.

She says no—big surprise. But then she whispers in his ear, and his mouth sort of drops open in this you're-such-a-bitch face. She smiles at him, then at me, grabs some slasher flick off the shelf, pays Pimple Boy behind the cash register, and then leaves. Before I have the chance to talk to her.

I grab a handful of utensils and a paper napkin and go to set them up in front of her, but the fork drops out of my hand, slides across the counter, and almost lands in her lap. Luckily she's able to catch it just in time. I'm such a total fuck-up.

"Sorry," I say. "I can get you another one."

"No, thank you," she says. "I prefer this one." She kisses the prongs and sets the fork down on the napkin.

I look at her place setting and notice I've given her

three extra spoons. I'm tempted to take them back, but maybe she won't notice. Maybe she'll even need three extra. I review all the spoonable items on the menu—soup, pudding, coffee, tea, grapefruit . . .

"Well?" she says.

"Well *what*?"

"Do you have a menu? I might like to order some food items."

"Right." I try to laugh it off and hand her one of the clean, laminated ones from under the counter. I don't know why I'm so nervous; usually I'm able to keep it cool around girls. I mean, I've been with *a lot* of girls before.

"How are you feeling today?" she asks.

Do I look sick? "Fine, and you?"

"*So* good." She swivels her seat back and forth, like the stool's a carnival ride or something, then makes one full spin around.

"We have some specials today." I flip to a fresh page in my order pad, trying my best to get my fingers to work right. I press the pencil point into the paper to stop the shaking, and look at her, and now *she's* the one staring at *me*. "What can I get you?" I ask.

"What were those specials again?"

Oh, yeah, the specials.

She lets out this girl-giggle, like it's no secret I'm completely sweatin' her. I can feel my face get all hot and red, and I'm trying my best not to laugh at myself.

"BLT with french fries and cole slaw for five fifty," I say, conscious that my eyes are welded to the goddamned ceiling. "Meat loaf with gravy, corn, and mashed for five ninety-nine. And spaghetti with meat sauce and meatballs for five twenty-five."

"Hmm . . ." She makes a face, like nothing I've told her sounds appetizing. "I might need a short interval to decide."

"Okay . . . sure." I turn around and face the cash register, pretend to type something in, feel stupid doing it, but end up ringing up a fried fish sandwich and a chocolate milk shake for the hell of it, then voiding it all out. My mother yells over to me, asks me what I'm doing, and suddenly I wish *I* was the one getting fried.

Calm down, I tell myself. Just talk to her. Just be cool.

I take a deep breath, tell my mom I'm all set, turn back around, and the girl is standing up, slinging that huge-ass purse over her shoulder, readying herself to leave. She smiles at me as she slides the menu between the salt and sugar shakers. But then this guy walks in, this Sean-guy from school, who, coincidentally, is now the boyfriend of that Kelly-girl I went to the party with. He comes up to the counter, and her eyes are all over him.

"Your aura has a murky haze," she says, grabbing at the crystal thing that hangs around her neck—this sticklike piece with points at both ends.

Sean gives her a weird look like he has no clue what

80

she's talking about, grabs a bunch of napkins from the dispenser, and blots them into the gash in his hand. Heinous.

"You're bleeding," she says, like it isn't completely obvious. She opens that big-mother purse of hers and takes out a long scarf.

"I'm all set," he says.

But she wraps the scarf around his palm anyway, changing the bloody napkins first, even getting some blood on her fingers.

What the hell was he thinking by coming in here? This isn't some drop-in clinic.

"Hey, Sean," I say. "I got a first-aid kit in the back. You wanna take it into the bathroom?"

But he ignores me, no surprise. The guy totally despises me. There was some stuff that went around after that party. Stuff about me and Kelly. Basically, I tagged her that night and she ended up wanting more. Like, relationship-more. I didn't want one then, but I wouldn't mind it now. Especially with this chick.

She finishes dressing the wound like she's Clara-fuckin'-Barton or something, and then cleans off her hand with a napkin and some ice water. "You'll have lunch with me, won't you?" she asks him. "I want to hear how you wounded yourself. How your aura got so murky." She holds on to the scarf-covered hand like she doesn't want to let him go, plops down on a stool, and signals for me to come and wait on her. "I'll have the garden salad with pocket bread," she says. "And an iced tea with lemon and honey."

"What can I get you, Sean?" I ask.

He ignores me again and turns to her. "Thanks for the scarf," he says, "but I gotta go. I gotta flat tire waiting for me outside."

"So, you don't want anything?" I say.

"You're a quick one," he says to me.

Fuck you, I smile, since the girl is here. I slap her order up on the turnstile, send it for a spin, and then go to make her drink. I slice a nice thick wedge of lemon, just the way I like it, stab it to the rim of her glass, and place her drink down in front of her.

It's been weird between me and Sean ever since he and Kelly started going out. We were never great friends, but at least we could talk every once and a while. I've wanted to say stuff to him about it, even tell him that I feel sort of bad about what happened.

Sean pitches a wad of napkins and then leaves. And the girl looks like she could cry.

"Thanks for helping him out," I say.

"He needs more help than a scarf."

No shit.

"Order up," my father calls from behind the grill. He pokes one of those plastic sword toothpicks into her pocket salad to make it look pretty, and then adds a sprig of parsley to the coleslaw. My dad knows me so well.

I decide to follow his lead. Decide I'm going to cheer this girl up, give her the complete LaPointe charm. This is my family's diner, for God's sake. I've got the home-court advantage. I can surprise her with dessert and fresh coffee, and even throw away the bill at the end. I take the plate and set it in front of her. "Anything else I can get for you?" I ask.

"No thanks, this looks delectable."

"So, do you go to school around here?" I ask.

"Yeah," she says. "The School of Mearl, ever hear of it?"

I shake my head.

"It's the one where you can sleep all day, slam poetry all night, howl at the moon, dance under the stars, feast on sweet conversation and a spicy ocean breeze—and bathing and clothing are optional." She takes the lemon wedge and sucks it like a tequila lime. "Wanna join?"

"Sign me up."

"Hi," she says, sticking her hand out. "I'm Mearl. That's pearl with an M." Then she laughs, withdraws her hand before I can shake it.

"Derik," I say.

"It's superb to meet you, Derik."

Superb. This girl is cool.

Aside from the few people that sit at my station, it's a pretty slow afternoon, and me and Mearl end up talking all through her lunch and through the Grape-Nuts custard I make her try.

"So you wanna set time together?" she asks me.

"Set time?"

"Yeah, you know . . . hang out for a while."

"Definitely." I give my dad the heads-up about what's going on. He doesn't care that I take off for a while. I think he's actually glad to let me go for the cause. He knows it's been kind of dry for me lately.

I ask her where she wants to go, and she tells me Danvers State. As in the hospital. As in the asylum.

"Why would you want to go there?"

"Because I want to see what it's like," she says. "Experience that space and all the old souls."

"You know it's closed."

"I know. I've researched."

"So no one's there anymore."

"Of course they're there. Just because there aren't actual physical people there doesn't mean the souls don't linger."

I know that I should run the other way. That in normal circumstances I would label her a freak and move on to the next, but these are no normal circumstances and this is no ordinary girl.

"Have you ever visited?" she asks.

"Yeah," I say. "I've been there once or twice. My friends and I broke in a couple times last year—to drink and hang out. Stupid stuff."

"Will you take me there?" she asks. And she's looking at me, into my eyes, like she really cares what I have to say. So how can I say no?

We hop into my truck, and we're talking and laughing about favorite superheroes and Cheez Whiz versus string cheese. And she's asking me questions and laughing at my jokes, like she really means it. Like she's really into me.

"Have you lived in Salem all your life?" she asks.

"Yeah. Pretty lame, huh?"

"Why is it lame?"

"I don't know. You've probably traveled around to some really great places."

"Yeah, but it isn't the same. I mean, growing up here, living in a city where the people have known you since forever . . . I think it's pretty luminous."

"Luminous?"

She nods like I get what she's saying.

"I don't know." I shrug. "I guess it's different if you've always been stuck here, you know, kind of boring."

"You're interesting, Derik." She licks the seal of a bubble gum cigarette and taps along the length to make sure it's closed.

"You're the one who's interesting." I position the rearview mirror to watch her. She pops the end of the cigarette into her mouth and blows, sending a puff of sugar smoke out the tip. The cigarette looks so good between her teeth, between those pale pink lips.

"How can a city with so many spirits be boring? I may have traveled around a bit, but I haven't truly ever rooted, you know?"

"Is that what you want to do? Root?"

I have no idea what I'm saying, and I'm pretty sure she knows it, too. She giggles at my lame response, scoots herself in toward me, and rests her head on my shoulder. She smells like cheese danish topped with coffee and whipped cream. And I just want to do everything right, more than I've ever wanted to do anything right in my life.

Fifteen minutes later, we're there. The abandoned hospital sits up on the hill, looking down at us. I pull around to the back so no one will see us, wondering where all the security guys are. But the place seems completely vacant today. As soon as the truck's in PARK, Mearl jumps out and starts running toward the cluster of brick buildings.

"Come on!" she shouts.

I sit there a moment, just looking at it and taking it in. It looks so different in the daytime. An abandoned hospital that doesn't quite know what it wants to be—an asylum, a gothic church, a school, someone's estate.

I get out and run toward her, up to the rear entrance. But for some reason, none of this feels right. It's different when you're drunk and stupid, and it's after two in the morning, and you can only see as far as your flashlight will let you. When your buddies tell you you're gonna find some pretty cool shit. But now, in the daylight, the sun shines on everything, and I'm forced to take it all in. The broken windows from angry fists. The overgrown brush crawling up the side like an escape route out, and the rusted bars and screens that keep you in.

She yanks on a side door, but it's locked. "How do we get in?"

I'm tempted to tell her I was too drunk at the time to remember, but before I can say anything, she takes my hands, kisses me on the mouth, and thanks me for bringing her here.

"Can't you feel it?" she whispers. "The energy? There's so much sadness here, but you and I . . . we can fix it." She smiles at me and studies my face, then kisses me again and pulls me close.

The next thing I know, I'm climbing up that ladder of overgrowth on one of the smaller buildings.

"Be careful!" Mearl shouts up to me.

I peek inside one of the windows near the top. The floor is littered with broken beer bottles, cigarette butts, and snack trash from late-night parties. I hoist myself up on the roof, thinking how much harder it is this time without extra hands to help pull me up. The vent we need to enter from is over to the left. I lay the grille to the side and slide down the duct.

It's dark inside, but light enough to see. I run through a connecting tunnel, toward the larger building. The stench of dank and dampness makes me want to hurl. When I finally make it to the other side, I take a wrong turn and end up in one of the patients' rooms. The walls are stained with red paint, splotched on to look like blood. And there's a graffiti sign over it all that says the room was painted with the blood of Mary Driscoll, some patient who lived here.

I kick through the debris. There are used condoms on the floor and pairs of dirty underwear, a whole heap. There's a Ken doll hanging from a noose in the center of the room and naked baby doll parts strewn everywhere— some with needles poked into the eyes and scalp; others with their dirty, rubbery arms and legs all knotted and mangled.

I look across the hallway into another room. I remember carving my initials into a wooden support beam in there, how me and Tom splashed yellow and green paint on the walls to make it look like lobotomy juice, and how me and Tammy Come-do-me, some freshman-wannabe-senior, made it all the way to third base in the hallway closet, and then to home plate in the parking lot.

It makes me wonder how the place looked the next day, in the light. If it looked like this. If Tammy woke up feeling like a senior.

I make my way into the hallway, hurry down a stair-case to unlock a back door, and let Mearl in.

"Thank you, Derik," she says, looking around.

The main room is big and dirty, and there are torn pages strewn all over the place, but I don't feel like reading them or seeing any more. Kevin, this kid from school, found an old patient's notebook in here one time and actually took it. He brought it to school and passed it around. It had all this fucked-up shit in it. There was this one entry in there about this woman, sitting in the audience on amateur night at this place, smiling like it was her freakin' birthday, but with blood pouring from her wrists, down the aisles. According to the notebook entry, one of the windows had broken and the orderlies hurried to pick up all the glass. They had put it together on a table like a puzzle, to make sure they got every piece. They didn't.

"This isn't right." Mearl is sweeping her arms through the air, pushing away the empty space around her, like she can see something I can't. "The spirits don't want me here. I'm sorry, Derik, but I don't feel right about this."

No shit. I take her hand and we leave, and head back to the truck. But, before I can haul ass out of there, the cemetery catches her eye and she has to experience that space, too. She makes me pull over so that we can see the graves. They're simply posts in the ground, marked with numbers.

"Do you see what happens when you have no roots, Derik?" she asks, thumbing over the point of her crystal pendant. "You have no identity. You become just a number. How can all these souls rest when they have no one to claim them?"

I put my arm around her and we walk back to the

truck. I want to ask about her family and where she's from, but I'm pretty sure she wouldn't know about either, so I just stay silent.

"I'm sorry I made you come here," she says. "I was just curious. I thought I might be able to do some good, you know? Help peel away the rust." She locks her door and then scoots in close to me. "It's so tragic—to be just a number."

"You're not just a number." I stroke her cheek, just a little, and say, "I think you're pretty great." And I really mean it.

She kisses me and rests her cheek against mine. "I want to know what it feels like to be from someplace. Not just some number. Not some unrested spirit without identity."

"What do you mean?"

"I mean I want to be with you. I want to experience it—your world of roots."

I feel kind of good bringing her to my house, showing her how nice it is, at the tip of a cul-de-sac overlooking all of Witchcraft Heights. We go inside and I ask her if she wants a drink, but all she wants is to see the inside of my room. So I take her there and she kicks off her shoes and barefoot-skates across my rug, all around my room.

"Having fun?" I ask.

She takes my hands and we spin around. At first I feel totally stupid doing it—but somehow with her, it's actually kind of cool.

"I think you're truly wondrous," she says. "And one day, when you put all that glitter out, and it's just you and your porous thoughts and your smashing ideas, I hope I still know you—an intelligent and harvesting young man. But for now, you're my karmic destiny."

We stop spinning and she kisses both my hands. And I know it's cheesy and totally unlike anything I've ever felt or thought before, but here, with this girl, after all this time, I just want to hold her and kiss her and never let her go.

"What's wrong?" she asks, when I don't say anything back.

And then I realize I can feel my face, stuck in some sort of confused knot. "It's just that nobody's ever said anything like that to me before," I say. "Wow, that just sounded so lame." What is the matter with me?

"It sounded honest, Derik. *Honest.*" She pats my hand. "Maybe you haven't let anyone get close enough to say those things to you."

"Not until now," I say. And I look at her. Really look at her, hoping she sees what I mean without my having to say it. Wondering if she'd care if I kissed her right now. I want more than anything to kiss her again.

"I'm happy you feel that way, Derik," she says. "Just think, if that Sean-guy hadn't come into your diner, we might never have shared like this."

"I'll have to thank him," I say, and she smiles at me, not breaking the hold I have on her eyes.

And I think she's right about being my destiny or me being hers. We were definitely meant to meet.

She goes and sprawls herself out on my bed, starts flopping around, telling me how wonderfully yellow everything is in here—even though my room is blue and gray. Then she stops, walks on her knees to the foot of the bed, and looks up at me like she could cry at any second. "Drink me up, Derik, for even just a short spell, and make this mine. My roots in the soil. Will you do that for me?"

Soil?

She gets up and makes a beeline for me. She plasters her lips to mine, thrusts her tongue in my mouth, yanks me onto the bed, and I go toppling on her.

She lifts my shirt up with her teeth. Then pulls it up and off, and I'm hoping she notices my body—my chest, my abs—the result of working out at a gym ten hours a week, but she's too busy unbuttoning my jeans, ripping them down with my boxers until they get stuck at my sneakers. She pulls off my shoes, and now it's just me, completely exposed, and her, exploring every inch of my body with her lips and tongue. She actually sucks *my* nipples.

I decide I should try and take her clothes off as well, but she pulls away when I touch her lacy sleeve. Instead, she stands up on the bed and gives me a striptease. First those sticks from her hair, so that the bun comes undone and her hair just falls, long and thick and wavy, like a mermaid. Then she peels off her top, and she's just got some bra-thing on underneath, and you can see right through it. She takes the straps down over her shoulders like they're suspenders, and rolls the thing down her waist, over her hips, off her legs, and then kicks it in my face. And she just stares at me, watching me watch her, like she can tell what I'm thinking—that she's the most unbelievable girl I've ever seen.

She blows me a kiss and then moves her fingers to the side of her skirt. She pulls at the ties, and the skirt just falls off her. Underneath she's wearing these silky boxer shorts, with hearts all over them, that make me laugh out loud. There's a pocket inside the hem. She reaches in, takes out a purple condom, and opens the wrapper with her teeth.

I lean back while she puts the thing on me, and it's really weird, but all of a sudden I can't help but think how I've never felt so close to a girl before, like she can read my mind and can be totally crazy, smart, and cool all at once.

She lays her naked body on mine, and already I'm holding back. "You're luminous, Derik," she whispers, leaning in to kiss my shoulder. But then I feel teeth—they sink into my skin, right beside my collarbone, completely catching me off guard, and so I let out a shriek. Lucky for me, I think my shrieking gets her going even more, because not two seconds later, she's circling her hips and letting out these catlike cries, right on top of me. I can't hold on much longer, so I try to distract myself and stare at the crystal stick around her neck, but it's bopping up and down right between her Mary

Janes, and so it's no use. Before I know it, I'm all done.

She rolls off and snuggles into my side. And I'm thinking that she liked it, that she's all set, because she's smiling at me, fingering through the gel in my hair, like nothing's wrong. Like she's completely satisfied.

"You're wonderfully crimson," she says.

And I want to say something totally incredible back. Not a line or anything bogus like that, but something smart and different and special. I want to tell her how awesome I think she is; tell her how this is so different for me, how it's crazy how it happened, the way we kept meeting, like it was meant to be; tell her that I've never felt this way about anybody before. But instead I say, "You're the one who's amazing." And then I lean over and kiss her lips, slowly, concentrating the whole time, hoping that it's full of the magical stuff they sing about in love songs, because it really feels that way for me.

When the kiss breaks, I lean into her ear and say, "Isn't it weird the way we kept bumping into each other?"

"What do you mean?"

"You know, the way we kept seeing each other. The party, Starbucks, the newsstand . . ."

"I don't know what you're talking about, Derik." She stops twirling her fingers through my hair. "We met *today*, at the diner."

"No, before, all those times. Even earlier today, at the video store."

"It must have been somebody else, Derik. I would

have remembered if I'd seen you before."

"Were you not in the video store today? Movie Mayhem? There was this old guy buggin' you."

"Yeah, I was there. But I didn't see you there. That's really unusual." She continues to nuzzle into my chest, but then there's this ringing from that enormous pocketbook of hers. "I should get that," she says, rolling over to answer it.

"Hello?" she says. "Hi. How are you feeling?" She grips the phone and moves toward the edge of the bed, like suddenly I'm in the way. "Truly wondrous," she continues into the phone. "No, nothing really. Just setting time with a friend. Sure. Yeah, I'd love to; that'd be crimson. I'll place there in an hour." She clicks her phone off and lies back down to give my nipple one final kiss. That's when she notices.

"You're bleeding," she says.

I look at my shoulder, noticing her bite marks, the way she broke right through my skin.

She grabs for a handful of tissues and presses them into my shoulder. "I guess I got a little carried away. I hope this doesn't change anything for you; it was a luminous time."

I grab the napkins from her, maybe a little too quick; I think she senses that I'm pissed. "I'm fine," I say.

Mearl responds by kissing my shoulder, then my chest. "Thank you, Derik," she whispers. "For letting me plant here, even if it was just to be uprooted again."

She sits on the edge of the bed with her back to me and slips on her bra-top thing and the lacy shirt. She pulls the heart boxers on, then wraps and ties her skirt, slides into her flip-flops, and swings the giant purse over her shoulder. Grabbing her hair sticks from the night table, she leans down next to me and whispers into my ear, just like she did with that perv at the video store. She tells me she's glad we met and wishes me a spiritually enlightened life.

And then she walks right out of it.

Sadie Dubinski

SATURDAY, AUGUST 12, 3:00 P.M.

I hate my house. I hate everyone inside of it. I even hate
the color—apple pie–filling brown, with globs of dirt stuck
to the bottom shingles. I'm standing at the front door,
but I don't want to go in. And I've already spent a whole
hour at the library. I wish Maria had let me stay at her
house, at least until after my mom went off to aerobics
class. I don't know why she didn't. I don't know why she
made me sneak out her bedroom window and hide in the
bushes. Or why she touched herself on her privates when
she changed her clothes. She told me not to peek, but I
did. And I almost wish I didn't.

My mom's car is parked in the driveway, so I know she's home. Maybe I'll just stay out here and play with my Game Boy, beat Dracula, free his prisoner, and become Sadie-istic, Supreme Vampire Huntress once and for all.

Except I'm hungry.

I turn the knob and push the door open. "Sadie," Mom says, coming out of the washroom. "Hi, sweetle-dee. I was just thinking about you." There's an unopened box of Nutty Buddies sitting on top of the heaping basket of clean laundry she's carrying. "Come on upstairs. Ginger and Nina have some friends over. We were just about to have a snack."

Is she really going to let me have one of those Nutty Buddies?

I follow her up the stairs and into the kitchen, glad she hasn't noticed that the sign she put on my shirt isn't there anymore.

Ginger, my bossy fourteen-year-old sister, stands in the middle of the kitchen floor showing her friend Cheryl how to do a proper plié. Ginger's wearing a dark, shiny red bathing suit that makes her look like a giant Fruit Roll-Up come to life. The snack key dangles from a long silver chain around her neck.

"A straighter back," Mom says. She slides the laundry basket onto the table and puts one hand on Ginger's bony shoulder and the other at the bottom of her spine. She guides Ginger down into the perfect plié, not even thinking about the Nutty Buddies just sitting there on top of the warm pile of laundry, probably melting at this very second.

Nina, my nine-year-old sister, sits at the kitchen table with her best friend, Douglas. They're playing Go Fish. "Hi, Sadie," she says, pairing up a couple of sevens.

"You've got a purple juice smile across your mouth," I say.

She shrugs and takes another sip of her Kool-Aid.

"Very nice," Mom says to Ginger. Ginger is able to plié down until her hair almost hits the floor. Her legs are long and tan. Almost as tall as my whole body. I wonder if my legs will be like that in three years, too.

But I don't look anything like my sisters. My hair is dark brown. Theirs is blond. They have blue eyes. My eyes are brown. They're both tall and skinny—even Nina is almost as tall as me. I need to lose sixteen pounds. Their skin is tan this summer. Mine is pasty white. They both like ballet. I have achilles tendonitis—which basically means that I pulled some muscles at the back of my heel—and so I can't do sports or dancing, and I have a doctor's note saying I can't do gym class. If the tendon tears completely, then Mom says I'll have to have surgery or my ankle and foot will kill even more.

I have one other sister, Kendra, who looks a little like me, but she decided not to come back from college this summer. When she came home last summer, Mom made her go to Weight Busters with us, complaining that she had gained the "freshman fifteen" from too much pizza and beer. Kendra is skinnier than me, but not as skinny as Ginger and Nina. I'm mad at Kendra for not coming home, even though I probably wouldn't have either. I can't wait till I go off to college and never have to come back.

"How about that snack?" Mom asks. She starts to open up the box of Nutty Buddies, but then stops and looks at me. "What happened to your sign?"

Ginger starts laughing. She clutches around her hollow stomach like it's the funniest thing she's ever heard. Cheryl starts laughing, too, and soon they can't even stand still. "You girls are so silly," Mom says, shaking her head.

They're laughing because of the sign. *The* sign. The one my mom pins to my shirt whenever I gain weight, or whenever I'm going out without her and she knows there's gonna be food. Or sometimes when I've eaten something I shouldn't. Or like today, when I have to go weigh in later. My mom says it's for my own good, that beauty is pain, and that someday I'll thank her. And then on comes the sign— just a normal piece of notebook paper that she's written on in big cursive letters: PLEASE DO NOT FEED SADIE.

I know I could take the sign off, and sometimes I do. But sometimes I forget it's even there. And sometimes I don't care if people see it.

Mom says the sign could be a lot worse. She says that when she was a teenager and trying to lose weight for the prom, she and her mother joined this weight-loss club that made members wear a pig nose, stand in the middle of a circle of people, and oink a bunch of times whenever they weighed in and had gained more than half a pound. I guess she's right. I guess that would be a lot worse.

"The sign fell off at Maria's," I say, plucking at my eyelashes, pulling out a three-lash fan.

"Why were you at Maria's?"

"She let me use her nail polish."

Mom looks at my Baby-Got-the-True-Blues fingernail shade and frowns. "Why is a seventeen-year-old hanging around with an eleven-year-old? You told me you were going to the park for arts and crafts."

"I was going to, but then I saw Maria."

Ginger and Cheryl are still laughing at me. Cheryl puffs out her cheeks, fat-girl style, and this makes Ginger laugh so loud and hard that her perfectly straight back slides down the wall and she collapses to the floor, holding her hand between her legs so she doesn't pee. Mom looks over at them. "Ginger, keep it up and Cheryl will have to go home and you'll have to go to your room." Then she turns back to look at me. "Did you have anything to eat?"

I shake my head.

"Well, let's have us a little snack and we'll talk about this later."

I nod and look at Nina. She smiles at me and scores another card from Douglas to make a pair of kings.

I hope she wins. I like her so much more than Ginger.

Mom busts open the side of the Nutty Buddy box with her thumb. She gives one cone to Douglas first. "There you go, sweetie," she says. One to Nina, one to Cheryl, and one to Ginger. Then she closes up the box and stuffs it in the freezer.

Mom puts her arm around my shoulder. "Now what do you say, you and me have our own snack?" She kisses the top of my head, and I want to cry so bad that my forehead hurts. I nod and look away, stare at the wallpaper, the stripes of pears and oranges and bananas, because I don't want anyone to see.

I look at the inside of the fridge, where Mom is pointing. "How about some nice carrot sticks? I bought some fresh yesterday at the farmer's market. And I have some yummy no-fat veggie dip."

"Okay," I say, hearing my own voice crackle.

She takes the package of carrots out, along with the container of dip. Ginger peels the paper off the cone part of her Nutty Buddy. She takes a bite and the cone is all chewy. I can see it in her mouth. I love it all chewy like that.

Mom arranges *our* snack on a Tupperware platter she bought from Maria's mother. She places the dip in the center and arranges the carrot sticks around it like sun rays. "Now, doesn't that look pretty?" She holds it out for everyone to look at.

No one says anything.

Me and Mom go out on the sunporch to eat, while Ginger and Cheryl move into the living room for more ballet, and Nina and Douglas keep playing cards. The sunporch is pretty new. It has a big yellow umbrella with pink flowers and matching cushiony lounge chairs. Me and Mom sit at the table, and she starts reading her book. It's a new one. The cover shows a man and a woman on horseback with their hair blowing, and mountains in the background. I wish we had that kind of breeze out here. It's so hot.

"You know, Sadie," Mom begins, "don't think I don't notice when Ginger isn't so nice to you. I'll speak to her later. I just didn't want to embarrass her in front of her friend. They're just silly girls. You'll be giggly like that one day, too. Everything will be funny."

"I don't think I'll ever be like Ginger."

"Ginger's metabolism is different than yours is. She lucked out. You didn't. *I* didn't. She got your father's genes. So did Nina. You weren't as lucky and got mine. So, like me, you just need to watch it, that's all."

"You look pretty to me."

"Thank you, sweetie. But Mom's gotta work very hard to look good. You know how hard I work. And I *still* need to lose at least ten pounds."

"I need to lose sixteen."

Mom smiles at me like she knows and feels bad about it. She leans forward and her dark wavy hair hangs into the dip. "Can you keep a secret?"

I nod.

"You'll be the lucky one in the end. I have friends who were like Ginger. They could eat whatever they wanted to growing up. They didn't have to count calories or carbs or fat grams. But then one day, poof, their metabolism slowed and they still kept on eating the same way, and now they're heavier than me. *Much* heavier. You and I *know* how to diet."

"You think one day Ginger will be fat?"

"Maybe. I wouldn't be surprised if her metabolism hasn't already started to slow. I've noticed her thighs are getting a bit heavy. If she doesn't watch it, she'll be joining us at Weight Busters, just like Kendra last summer. Remember?"

The thought of Ginger at one of our Weight Busters meetings makes me smile. I picture a fat Ginger stepping barefoot onto the scale, the seams of her Fruit Roll-Up bathing suit stretched, flab bulging out all over. But then Mom pops my fantasy bubble, "You know you have to weigh in tonight," she says.

How could I not know? She's reminded me like, a KAGILLION times.

"Stop picking at those pretty lashes, honey," she says. "You're not gonna have any left." Mom reaches over to grab a carrot, dunks it in the chunky white dip, and then stuffs it into her mouth. She smiles at me between chews, and I almost feel better.

Except I don't want to eat carrots. But I'm so hungry I'll eat almost anything. I take one from the sun ray arrangement, and now it looks like a white face with wild orange hair that sticks out straight. I think about telling her this but change my mind when she turns a page in her book. I drop my carrot into the dip, push it down with my finger, and then spoon it back up. It's completely covered and so are my fingers. I try a bite. It tastes like crunch, cold nothing. I leave the rest in my napkin.

I want a real snack.

I get up from the table and go back inside. Nina's still in the kitchen with Douglas. I could pretend to go into the freezer for some ice for a drink and take a Nutty Buddy instead, but I'm too afraid Nina will see and tell on me. Plus, it's kind of hard to hide an ice-cream cone in a tennis outfit with just Tinker Bells all over it, no big pockets or anything.

Ginger's just around the corner, in the living room. I know *she* would tell. She's showing Cheryl her frappés now. Cheryl looks so bored. She's sitting on the ottoman, but she looks like she might fall asleep. I look at Ginger's thighs. Mom's right, they are getting kind of round. I smile, then start to laugh.

"What?" Ginger says, when she sees me spying on her.

"Nothing." I laugh.

"Well, then leave us alone. Go bother Nina."

"Guess what I did today," I say.

"I don't care what you did."

"O-kay-ay," I sing. "If you don't want to know what I did at Ma-ri-a's . . ."

Ginger smacks her foot back down on the floor, making the china in the hutch tremble. "I don't care what you did. I don't know why you hang around with that freak. I don't know *why* Mom lets you."

"She's my friend."

"You don't have friends."

"Neither do you!" I shout.

"Who do you think *this* is?" She points at Cheryl. "LEAVE US ALONE. GO BOTHER NINA!"

I feel my cheeks get hot. Cheryl is staring at me. They both are, waiting for me to turn around and leave so they can talk about me. Cheryl copies my sister by putting her hands on her hips. I hate Cheryl, too.

"Mom says you have fat thighs, FAT-SO!" I shout. Then I walk past them and down the hall as fast as I can. I slam my bedroom door shut and belly flop onto my bed.

I hate Ginger! I hate her! I hate her! I hate her!

I take the Game Boy out of my skirt pocket and continue where I left off, in one of the castle's corridors, just about to use a clock and create a fire-whipping spell that would bring those vile dragon zombies to my mercy. I hate those evil dragon zombies!

Five minutes later, there's a knock on my door. "Sadie?" Mom comes in. "I'm taking Ginger, Nina, and their friends to the beach. Do you want to come, sweetle? Put on your suit. We'll take a quick swim."

"I don't know," I say, collecting an action card. "My foot is kind of hurting me."

"Well, the cold water might do it some good." I peek up at her. She's already wearing her swimsuit. The purple one with the skirt—the one that has mega-huge silver-and-gold flowers on the waist.

"Hurry up, Sadie," Ginger says, poking her head in. "I don't have *all* day. I have to go babysit later." She's wearing a pair of sunglasses, really tiny ones, with pink tinted glass that barely covers her eyeballs. And she has her ballet-slipper beach towel draped over her arms.

The snack key is gone from around her neck.

I look at her and Mom, and then at Cheryl, who's standing in the hallway, in a teeny yellow bikini, and I say, "I think I just want to stay home and put my foot up."

"Oh, honey, are you sure?" Mom asks. "We won't have as much fun without you. Will we, girls?"

Ginger gives Cheryl the "okay-sure" sign with her fingers.

"Yup. I'm sure," I say.

"Come on, Mom," Ginger says. "Let her stay."

"Okay," Mom says finally. "We'll only be an hour or so. I want to get back for aerobics, and I have to drop Ginger off at the Pickerels'. Then we're going to weigh in. Daddy won't be home from work until after eight, so we'll probably have a late, light dinner. Okay, sweetle-dee. Don't forget."

107

"Okay," I moan. I'm old enough to stay home by myself. I'm *not* a baby.

She leans forward. "Oh, and if you want something to eat, there's more carrots in the fridge." She pauses, and her eyes get wide and pointed, like this is charades and she's a giant human purple-painted exclamation point. I know she's not *just* talking carrots. I know she's afraid I'll cheat.

"Yup." Just go! I hate all of you!

"Okay, so call me on the cell phone if you need me. We're just going down to Forest River." She closes the door and I wait to hear them leave. To hear them pack up (I'm sure) a carrot-less cooler of treats. To herd down the stairs and then run back up because Nina forgot to grab the sunblock. And then finally to close and lock up the front door. That's my cue. I save my place in Castlevania, hop off my bed, peer out the window, and watch them get in the car. Nina and Douglas in the back. Mom, Ginger, and Cheryl in the front.

Me, at home, alone. Free.

The car backs out of the driveway and turns down the street. I head into the kitchen. I open up the freezer, and a puffy cloud of freezer air hits my face. It feels good. I look around for the box of Nutty Buddies, but there's just packages of frozen stuff—boxes of green beans and orange squash, a stack of hamburger patties with the paper in between, and lots of Reynolds Wrapped stuff.

No ice cream.

I look harder. They must be in here somewhere. Maybe Mom hid them. Maybe they're stuffed way in the back. Maybe I should empty out the freezer.

I move the step stool over and start filling my arms with frozen stuff. Then I stack it all up on the table. Some of this stuff is really heavy. Mom's stocked up on a trillion packages of frozen chicken and about a kazillion turkey pies. I think I see a container of something chocolate in the back. I move the broccoli spears and the square blocks of frozen pea pods to get at it, take it out, but see that it's a container of liver. I pry the cover off to be sure. Touch the icy pieces. Brown and bloody and frozen, like the remains of one of Dracula's victims after an ice blizzard. *So gross!*

There's a ball of aluminum foil in the back. It has a tiny wedge of brown sticking out from its Reynolds Wrap. I take the piece out. Ice dots the side, but it looks like chocolate for sure. I unravel it and see that it's cake. Mom and Dad's wedding cake. I remember Dad showing it to me right before their anniversary a couple years ago. It's one of the rose pieces. A white rose, made with butter cream.

I look back in the freezer. It's practically empty. No Nutty Buddies. No nothing.

I might as well eat the cake.

I lick the rose part first. It's so cold; it barely has any flavor. The sides of the cake are frozen with ice crystals, and you can't exactly suck cake like a Popsicle. I decide to put it in the microwave.

I stand right in front until the beep, take it out with my fingers, and then plop it onto a napkin. It's steaming. There are curls of smoke that rise from the frosting. I break off a piece of the rose part, a mouthful of chocolate cake underneath, and finger it into my mouth. At first it's so hot I can barely taste anything. But then it kind of melts over my tongue, and all I taste is . . . freezer, like I've filled my mouth with old and yucky frost.

It's too gross to even swallow, even *with* the sugary rose, so I spit it out in one marbleized ball, put what's left back in the aluminum foil wrapping, and stuff it way back in the freezer. There's no way Mom and Dad would have eaten that anyway.

I cram the frozen stuff back into the freezer as best I can. At first, I try to put it all back the way I took it out, but everything starts to look the same, just a bunch of giant tinfoil balls mixed with white and green boxes. Mom probably won't even be able to tell the difference. I go to shut the freezer door, but it won't close. There's too much stuff jammed in. I rearrange one tinfoil blob with another, shift the squash with the frozen asparagus box. Still no luck. There's one giant tinfoil brick, a frozen meat loaf, I think, that keeps me from shutting the door.

I push it in, hard, jam my shoulder against it, hold it in place, and whip the door closed before it can fall out. Yes!

I check the clock. It's 4:05. Mom and them have been gone for about a half hour. I should have at least another hour before they come home. I ballet-toe down the hallway into Ginger's room, reminding myself how she wasn't wearing the snack key when she left. I expect to have to search through all her stuff—between the mattress, under her pillow, taped behind the headboard. But it's right there, lying on the dresser, in her ballerina tutu–shaped jewelry dish. Ginger's so dumb, even dumber than Dracula's ghouls leaving all those rings and magical potions lying around the castle.

I take it and head downstairs—to the place where my treasure lies. The snack cabinet and fridge.

The snack quarters are way in the back, beyond the washroom and Dad's office. I ballet-toe through both. I can do ballet way better than Ginger. Mom tried to get me into Dance-tastic once, that's the good group, but my achilles tendon started acting up during tryouts, so I didn't make it. Dance-tastic's the group Ginger's in, but I think she only made it because Mom helps out at all the recitals and helps make the costumes and stuff. Plus, Ginger didn't even get a callback at the auditions for the *Nutcracker* in Boston last year. Everybody who's at least a little good gets a callback.

I make it on tiptoes all the way into the snack room. And just being in here, when I'm not supposed to be, and no one's home, and it's so quiet, just me and the hum of the fridge, makes me feel like I'm in one of the dark hallways of Castlevania, and at any minute one of Dracula's blood-feasting ghouls, or maybe even Dracula himself, if he dares, is going to jump out at me. *I love it!*

No question, I go for the fridge first. It's one of those double ones with the doors that open up from the middle. There's a hingelike metal thing on the doors, with a padlock. I insert the magic key and it comes undone pretty easily. I open up the freezer part, and there, lying atop the ice-cream sundae bars, are the Nutty Buddies.

The Nutty Buddies!

My treasure for being such a good player. I grab the box, and I'm so excited and my fingers are all tingly I can barely get them to work right. There are two ice creams left. Just like I thought. Six to a box and four already eaten.

But Mom would definitely notice if I took one.

Or . . . maybe she might think that it was Ginger who ate it. Or Nina. Nina sometimes uses Ginger's key. Maybe Nina got another one for Douglas. Douglas *is* a growing boy, as Mom sometimes says. Or maybe Ginger could have given the key to Cheryl to get another. Even Dad likes to have an ice cream once in a while in the summer.

I take one out, look down at it, feel the soft cone beneath my fingers. I'll just say I don't know *who* ate it.

I tear off the paper that covers the ice cream part and mash my lips against the nutty topping. The shell-like fudge is cold against my teeth, but I'm able to bite a big piece of it off, so big that it fills my mouth wide and sticks out a little. I press the chocolate into my tongue with the roof of my mouth, breaking it up, slurping the piece before it changes into syrup, and I swallow it up.

I take another bite. The vanilla ice cream swirls inside my mouth. I play with it at the tip of my tongue, press my lips together, feel it against the roof. So cold. I swallow it down fast. The bloodthirsty ghouls will probably be home soon.

The cone part is just the way I like it. Soft and chewy. I have to pull at it with my teeth, but then I get a little piece of the paper wrapping in my mouth. I try to chew it free, but I can't quite do it unless I want to spit everything out. I swallow it all down instead, rip the rest of the paper off, and then bite across the whole cone so that the ice cream leaks out the sides and I have to lick it up quick. Then I put my mouth over the entire top and suck. And one giant ice-cream ball shoots into my mouth and lands at the back of my tongue. So good. Better than anything.

I poke the cone's point into my mouth and chew down on it, eyeing the last Nutty Buddy in the box. I grab it, tear the paper from the top, and start all over again.

When the Nutty Buddies are gone, I take a breath and see that I'm still standing in front of the open freezer, the cold air blowing in my face. All of a sudden, I don't feel so good. Not sick, but there's a weird tightness in my chest when I breathe. I can't think and I don't know what to do. I don't know if I should lock the fridge back up and go upstairs. If I should risk all my Weight Buster points and have some ice-cream sandwiches. Or just take a peek in the snack cabinet.

I decide on the cabinet since I don't really want any more ice cream anyway. I can bring the snack treasures I find up to my room and hide them before everyone comes home.

I move toward it, hold the key out, but my fingers are shaking. They're hovering around the lock the way the night moths do at the spotlight in front of our house. Maybe I shouldn't do it. Maybe I should just go back upstairs. I feel my face scrunch up, my chest get tighter. Mom and her vampire clan will probably be home any minute now. There probably isn't time.

But I have to. Today I have the key. Tomorrow Ginger will hide it in the fortress, someplace good. Someplace I won't be able to find it. She was in a rush today, to go to the beach; tomorrow she won't be.

It takes my jittery fingers a couple times to get the key into the lock. But then they do, and I turn the key, and the lock comes undone, and for some reason my chest relaxes and I'm able to breathe again.

Just like the fridge, the cabinet doors swing open from the middle. I grab the handles and pull wide, arms outspread like a mighty, immortal bird. The shelves are full of treasures. Anything I want. Twinkies, barbecue chips, Fudge Stripes. An eight-pack of snack-size Dorito bags, a fresh can of Sour Cream & Onion Pringles, peanut butter–filled pretzels.

I seize the Twinkie box and hold it under an arm,

giggle at the thought of *seize*, one of my English vocab words. Luckily it's already been opened. There are six Twinkies left. I take three of them so that the box looks sort of full. Then I *seize* the long sleeve of Doritos and take out two bags, still leaving a few *up the sleeve*. I giggle at my lame little joke. I'm dying to take a stack of the Pringles, but since the can isn't open, it'd be way too risky. I tell this to myself, and yet I can't seem to move, like maybe there's a chance. Maybe Mom will just think someone else opened it.

I think about tearing the silver seal off just enough and then gluing it back on when I'm done. I'm sure Dad has a glue stick in his desk. Or maybe Mom might just think the can was opened by someone in the grocery store. We've both seen the trails of hungry shoppers leaving empty cookie and chip packages between two-liter bottles of Coke. I'll take just a small stack. It'll be perfect. No one will notice.

I take the can out, and my hands are too full. I need to put my stuff down. Maybe on the bottom step of the staircase. I make my way toward it, my arms full of all my delectable treats, and then I hear something. At the front door. Through the tiny square windows at the top, I can see the screen door swing open.

They're home!

My heart squeezes so tight I can barely breathe. I can't even move. My throat feels like it's closing up, filling with Nutty Buddy ice cream.

"Sadie!" Nina shouts, throwing the front door open, then closed. She looks at the snacks in my hands and then turns back around to lock the door. "RUN! Upstairs. Now! They're coming!"

I run upstairs as fast as I can, crushing my snack treasures into my chest, feeling like some wicked vampire with long yellowy nails and teeth is going to plant those nails right into my back and then suck the blood right out of me if I don't go quick enough.

I make it into my room, kick the door shut, stash the treasures under my bed, and then hide in my closet, in the back, under my nest of Hello Kitty winter covers, my protective cloak of armor. I pull at my eyelash hairs one by one, until I'm able to catch my breath.

Maybe my ally Nina will be able to clean up the snack room before anyone else sees it. Maybe Mom and her evil assistant Ginger are having one of their heart-to-hearts outside, and that's why Nina came in first. They still have to unpack the car, and that takes time. With each thought I feel a little better. My heart is able to unclench. But then my bedroom door is thrown open, the heavy wood slamming against the wall, probably making another mark.

"SADIE!" Mom yells.

I scrunch up ball-tight under the armor and make sure my head is covered completely. I hear my treasures, the bags of Doritos, being thrown across my room, that familiar crinkle sound.

"Sadie!" she yells again. I can tell she's right outside the closet door now. "I know you're in there. Come out NOW! Or I'll make you come out."

I don't do anything. I can't. My chest is going in and out so fast it's hard to breathe.

"Fine!" She slides the door open so that it slams into the pocket like one of Dad's eight balls. She grabs my arm, covered in armor. "Take your thumb out of your mouth. You're not a baby anymore."

I think I'm going to faint, but then I cry out—one long, loud wail.

She pulls me to my feet. I hold the armor to my face for as long as I can before she tugs it away. But still I don't look at her. I'm just crying and my foot starts hurting. She pulled too hard.

"You are grounded!" she shouts. I can hear the clench of her venomous teeth. "No playing with friends. No going to the park. No TV. No snacks."

"NO!" I cry back.

"I want *you* to go into the kitchen NOW and put the freezer back the way you found it. Did you eat anything?"

"No!"

"Are you lying to me?"

"No!"

"If you're lying to me, I'll know. Everyone will know tonight when you go weigh in. They're going to be so disappointed in you."

I feel sick. I feel like I can't breathe, like there's glass stuck in my chest, like all the doors are slamming in my head. And my ankle and foot are aching, all the way up my leg. "I don't feel good," I say. "My achilles tendon hurts." I bend my leg to get the weight off it.

"Too bad."

"No," I cry. "You hurt it."

Mom grabs me by the arm and pinches my skin. "Pick up the junk food. NOW!" she shouts.

I do, but it's hard to fit it all in my arms. I keep dropping bags of Doritos. There's a Twinkie behind the door. Mom doesn't see it and I don't point it out.

She drags me down the hallway, past Hideous Ginger and her point-taking clone, Cheryl, and into the kitchen.

"Thanks for stealing my key, thief," Ginger says. She opens the Pringles, takes out a three-stack, inserts them into her smiley mouth, and chews and chews and chews. "Yummy, yummy. Want one, Cheryl?" Ginger holds the container out to Cheryl, but Cheryl just looks at me and shakes her head.

I hate Ginger *so* much. So much I want to just rip her eyes out and feed them to one of Dracula's pet rats.

The kitchen's too bright. The light stings my eyes. I try to keep them shut, but Mom grabs my face and makes me look. The freezer door is open: a bunch of frozen stuff is lying on the ground. It must have toppled out.

She pulls me by the arm over to the sink and makes

me open up all the Twinkies and Doritos. I stand on the step stool and collect it all into a nice little mound, the Twinkies at the bottom, across the hole so they don't fall in, the Doritos on the top and sides like a sandcastle.

"Now turn the faucet on."

I choose the hot water and watch it drill down into my snacks, making them fall apart and plop into the hole. Mom turns on the garbage disposal and it eats everything up, even lets out a burp in the end.

"Not so appetizing now, is it?" she says.

I shake my head, and the steam from the burp rises up through the hole to kiss my face. What a waste!

"Now I want you to rearrange the freezer—put everything back exactly the way you found it. Hear me?"

"Can I help her?" Nina asks. She's peeking at me from the hallway.

"NO!" Mom says. "Go play in your room. Tell Douglas to call his mother to pick him up."

"How come Cheryl gets to stay?" Nina asks.

But Mom doesn't answer. She grabs a picture off the fridge, a heart that Nina drew, flips it over, grabs the dry-erase marker from the board, and writes—PLEASE DO NOT FEED SADIE. SHE IS A BAD GIRL WHO CHEATS ON HER DIET. Then she staples it to my front, over Tinker Bell's face. I'm crying now, so hard I wish I was dead. I wish I would just die.

Mom ignores my crying and heads to her room—I'm

sure—to change into her stupid red-and-white candy-cane aerobics leotard. Nina stomps down the hallway and slams her door shut, leaving Douglas to sit by himself in the living room.

And now I'm all alone in the kitchen. I pause to pluck out a nub of lashes, but when I look down, see a smear of watery blood on my fingertips. I touch the lid to be sure. More blood. And the skin feels sore and puffy. At first I feel myself shaking. Feel my heart break up into bits of splintery glass. But then I close my eyes and tell myself to relax, to be strong. There's bound to be bloodshed at this level. What's important is that I finish the game.

I grab a couple Reynolds Wrapped packages and throw them into the garbage. Then I remember Mom and Dad's cake sitting at the back of the freezer. It goes next.

Feeling a little better, I blot at my eye with a napkin, grab my magic whip, and sneak down the stairs. I open the front door as quietly as I can, careful not to disturb any of the wakeful beasts of the lair. I scooch myself through the crack and out the screen door.

And now I'm out. I'm free. I've won this level.

I run across the driveway and down the street as fast as I can. Away. I know I'll get in trouble later. I know I've probably used up all my magic meter. That I'll probably be grounded for a month and have to wear this stupid sign pinned to my clothes for the next year, but at least it's not the pig nose, and at least I got that ice cream.

Robby Mardonia

This is just a little too real for me.
I did love you. Just not anymore.
I'm sorry, Robby.

I can see her running down the sidewalk, that yellow
sundress whipping up in the back with each stride. But I
can't chase after her. I won't. Even if it kills me. I will sit here
and count as high as it takes, will picture a boy and his dad
flying kites by the seashore, but I will not go after her.
Will not beg her forgiveness for whatever I did wrong:

Should I have brought flowers? A poem? Maybe I shouldn't have hugged her like that right away. I will not force her to listen to my side. I clench my fingernails into the vinyl booth seat and promise myself this over and over. And over. Until I can finally take normal breaths.

With a glass of ice water, I swallow down the image of Kelly running away from the diner, away from me, and I'm able to unclench my fingernails. I think I'm sweating, that it's visible all over my face. I take a napkin from the dispenser and wipe at my forehead and the back of my neck. The waitress, a pudgy, pimply, straight-out-of-band-practice misfit, is looking at me weird, like she's scared for me.

Maybe I'm scared for me, too.

She holds one side of her tangerine-colored hair back and reinserts a red silk flower, smiling at me the whole time, like she wants to come over. I take another sip of ice water to ward her off, like maybe she'll leave me alone if she sees me eating and drinking. I pick up my fork and poke at the sausage links.

"How are you doing?" she chirps, standing over me now, head to knee in pink-and-white waitress garb.

"Fine." I fork-slice off the butt-end of the sausage link.

"More coffee?"

"No thanks."

"Are you sure? You look like you could use a little perking from the percolator." She laughs at her ridiculous pun, flings the rag she's holding over her shoulder, and heads toward the counter to get a fresh pot.

I puncture my fork into the sausage and put it up to my mouth, feel it on my lips—pickled with grease, hot and bumpy. The spicy steam—a blend of fried pork, black pepper, cumin, and garlic—hits against my upper lip, reminding me of Sunday brunches after church five and a half years ago, the way my mother used to make them.

Five and a half years since homemade sausages. Five and a half years of thinking about them, pretending it was them in my mouth, on my tongue, and between my teeth, instead of lukewarm cereal, undercooked toast, and still-frozen-in-the-middle, sorry-excuse-for sausages. And yet, I can't even take a bite. Don't even want them now.

"Are you from around here?" The waitress is back. She fills my mug up with steaming black coffee and then reaches into her apron pocket to throw down four or five of those mini plastic creamers.

I nod, tearing the lid off one of them and adding it to my mug.

"Oh, yeah? Where?" She's one of those girls who wears her lipstick bright Christmas-bow red and too big on her lips, as though she's not looking in a mirror when she applies it, or she wants to give the illusion of a bigger mouth, or I don't know what. Maybe it's just me. Maybe that's the new rage and I've just been away for too long.

And yet, Kelly looked perfect. In that yellow sundress.

With, I'm sure, underneath, the pink bra and panties I asked her to wear.

"I *used* to live around here," I say, hearing a twinge of annoyance in my own voice. I take the spoon and stir the cream, keeping my eye on the swirl, counting the number of stirs until the two liquids become one.

"Oh," she says, deadpan, as though she hears the annoyance, too. But instead of moving away, she simply stands there, coffeepot in hand.

I fork off a corner of my omelet and rake through the melted orange cheese inside.

"Was that your girlfriend who left? Bummer, huh? She looked pretty peeved."

I glance over at Kelly's place setting, at the pale-pink lipstick stain she left on her coffee cup, and feel the urge to put my mouth over it.

"I hate it when me and my boyfriend get in a fight," she continues. "Actually, he's not really my boyfriend any-more. We sort of broke up. He says I'm too young for him, but he doesn't know what he's talking about. A soon-to-be sophomore in high school who already knows what she wants out of life is *way* more mature than a senior who doesn't, don't you think?" She looks down at the plate of untouched pancakes Kelly left and presses her lips together in a scowl. "He'd do something like that—just stomp out in the middle of breakfast—without even talking it out."

I make a checked pattern with the melted cheese and

start counting up the blocks I've created within its grid. Twenty-six.

"At least that means more breakfast for you, right?" She laughs. "That is, if you like peanut-butter pancakes."

I detest this girl.

"I hate peanut butter," she continues. "It's so icky; the smell . . ."

I look up at her, at her foolish little face, the spray of orange freckles across the bridge of her nose, and those rosy fucking cheeks. "I'm really hungry," I say. I take a giant bite of sausage to show enthusiasm for my food, and chew nice and big and happy so she gets the message. I think she does. Her sloppy red lips melt down at the corners like a sad clown face, and for just a millisecond she looks almost scared. Her eyes still pressed on my chewing, she takes a couple steps back and then turns around to leave me be. Finally.

I finish up what's left in my mouth, but I really want nothing more than to spit it out. I reach over to take Kelly's cup. I place my mouth over the lipstick spot and imagine her kiss. Soft and warm and slow. I feel my tongue edge out against the ceramic and have to stop myself, have to open my eyes. Luckily nobody's watching.

I look out the window once more, to see if maybe she changed her mind and came back. But she isn't there. Isn't spying at me from behind a parked car or street pole; isn't hoping that maybe I'm still here, waiting for her to come back. I grab a fresh napkin and pull a pen from the front pocket of my shirt.

Dear Kelly,

It looks like we're back to letter writing again. I'm sorry if you got weirded out. I guess that's normal. But you never should have come to meet me if you didn't mean it about loving me, or if you were only playing around, like this is some make-believe game. It's real for me and I'm sorry if it's "too real" for you, but you made it real by coming here, after five and a half years of just letters and photographs. I love you, Kelly, and I know you love me, too. Don't be scared. Life is scary, but it'll be safer together.

Love,
Robby

P.S. I wish you had given me your father's number or address. I'll be here every day, same time, same booth, waiting for you. Please come for me.

I read the note a couple times, trying to decide if it

sounds too harsh, if it covers everything. I lean back against the vinyl seat and review my intentions, what I want her to understand in my words. I want her to know that I'm hurt, that I love her, that she's all I've been thinking about—that what's gotten me through the past five and a half years of prison without killing someone else or even myself is the faith that one of her letters would be coming. The thought of reading her words, imagining her whispering them into my ear, feeling the heat of her breath on my neck like hot, steamy tea.

I *don't* want her to be angry at me, nor do I want to hurt her. I just want her to realize that she's made a terrible mistake.

My head suddenly feels fuzzy. Maybe I'm thinking too hard. Maybe I just need to take a break, forgive myself for whatever mess I've made with Kelly, and clean it up as best I can.

I fold up the napkin and slide out from the booth seat. The waitress is hovering over the counter, talking to some guy in army fatigues.

"Miss?" I call.

She holds her hand out, as if to stop traffic, and says, "Just a sec," not taking her eyes off the army guy. She cups around his ear and whispers something. And suddenly I want nothing else but to be him for a second— to be the one being whispered to and breathed on. I touch my neck, still feeling where Kelly had breathed only minutes before, when we first hugged hello.

The waitress draws away, and the two of them laugh at whatever she's said. I'm so into the moment, I almost laugh, too, have to catch myself. The army guy stands up from his stool and waves her good-bye. Her eyes stay hooked on him until he's out the door, until those annoying door bells jingle his exit.

"You want your check?" she asks, finally looking at me.

I shake my head. "I want to know what you said to that guy."

"It wasn't anything about you." She turns her back on me to take up the guy's dirty plate.

"I just want to hear it," I say.

She stops, looks at me, and then lets the edge of the dirty plate smack down against the linoleum counter. "You didn't seem so itchy to hear me just a few minutes ago."

"I am now." I suck my lips in, hopeful, but then feel myself start to shake.

"I don't think so." She feeds the dirty plate into the sink.

"Please . . ." Is my upper lip perspiring? I wipe it to be sure. A slight sudation.

Her face scrunches up as though I'm not making sense, like she doesn't understand. "I'll get your check and then maybe you should go. Your girlfriend's probably missing you." She glances back at the cook, some middle-aged guy with at least fifty pounds on me. He nods to her.

Now I'm really shaking. I think I've scared her and I'm not sure how or why. I just know that I need to leave. I flip a twenty dollar bill out of my wallet, slap it on the counter, and head out the door, without even mentioning my plan to leave the note for Kelly in case she comes back.

Instantly I feel better, more in control, like I did the right thing. The fresh California breeze wraps around my body like a warm towel. I breathe it in and push it out, able to calm the jangling nerves inside me.

I take a seat on one of the benches across the street. I don't want to leave quite yet, just in case Kelly comes back.

"Robby?"

I turn around. But it isn't Kelly. It's her. The waitress.

"I think you left something." She hands me the napkin with my note on it. "Kelly must be really special. I'm sorry if I got the wrong idea and thought you were some jerky. You're obviously super sad. I know I'd be totally spazzing if my guy ditched me after waiting five and a half years to see him." She comes and sits next to me on the bench, still in her pink-and-white waitress attire. "Were you in the army or something?"

"Aren't you going to get in trouble with your boss?"

"He let me off early. It's *so* dead in there."

She plucks a package of some sort from the front pocket of her dress—some kind of candy. "Wanna lick?"

she asks, removing the wrapper and sliding the ring-pop onto her finger. There's a big candy jewel on the top. "It's cherry." I shake my head and she brings it to her mouth for a suck. "So, what's your day like?" she asks.

"I don't know," I say, just realizing it myself. My only plan for the past two years has been spending my life with Kelly.

"Wanna hang out?" She kicks her feet, in these heavy black shoes, back and forth in the dirt. "I'm Joy, by the way." She extends her hand to admire the candy jewel and then gives it another good suck.

"Robby."

"Yeah, I know, remember?" She smiles and points to the napkin note cradled in my palm. "So, wanna?"

A part of me feels like I should stay and wait for Kelly. I *know* Kelly. She'll realize what a mistake she's made and come try to find me. She'll feel her panties clutching her upper thighs, warming her skin, and know I'm a part of her. I just hope she remembers the name of the motel I'm staying at. "Maybe not," I say finally.

"Come on." She gets up and tugs my arm. "If you're good, I'll tell you what I whispered in Duggan's ear."

"Duggan?"

"The guy at the counter."

I smile at the mere thought of it—of her, breathing on my neck, having it be slow and rhythmic and hot. "Just a walk," I say.

"Cool!" she squeals.

We end up walking by my old school since it's only about ten minutes away. It just seems natural to walk that way, like, even though my life's been set to fast-forward and everything has changed, there's a part of myself still resigned to old habits.

"This is where I go to school," she says. "I can't wait to get out. I already know what I want to be in life. I wish I could go to one of those high schools that are like college, you know, for kids who already got it figured out. Not a vocational school, but one of those alternative places where you live away and cook your own meals and stuff. But my parents want me to go the traditional route. You know, four years of high school, four years of college, two years working, then marriage, blah, blah, blah. Do you want to know what I want to do?"

I already regret letting her tag along with me. Why did I? Is having her whisper in my ear really worth it? I look at her mouth, smiling at me, white teeth against such lipstick-red lips. A tongue that peeps out between the bite. "Yes," I say aloud.

"Okay, but don't laugh," she says. "I want to be a princess. I know what you're thinking. I know it must sound totally lame, like a fairy tale, but I want to reinvent the word princess. I mean, what makes people *royal*? People make people royal, *right*? It's humans who invented the whole concept, *right*? They may have been kings or queens or knights or whatever, but they were still *human*. So why can't another human change it? Update it? You shouldn't have to marry or be born into it. Isn't the American dream based on the fact that we can do and be whatever we want? I'll be an American princess. I'll be a role model for young girls."

"I know this path behind the school," I say. "It leads to Capers Pond. Do you want to walk up there? It'll be pretty this afternoon. Lots of shady trees. We can pick wild-flowers if you want."

Her face falls as though disappointed I chose not to comment on her puerile idea of a vocation. I say, "I think you'll make a very fine princess."

"Really, Robby?" She crosses her arms and twirls around on one foot, like a ballerina, but then fumbles and nearly trips over her own feet. I wonder why she elects to wear her waitress uniform as everyday street attire. And suddenly I get a vision of her hustling to the bus stop as a prepubescent schoolgirl—schoolbooks loaded in her back-pack, boys kicking dirt up at her from behind, a kick-me sign taped to her back.

"Do you really think it might be possible?" She smiles again, thirsty for my acceptance. "I mean, normally princesses have to be really, really pretty. And I know I'm reinventing the word and everything, but *still*."

I nod and manage to smile back.

"I'll have to change my last name, though. You wanna know what it is?"

Before I can feign interest, she blurts it out—Ryder. Joy Ryder. Something about her father's motorcycle.

"But I have it all planned out," she says. "I'll just put Van in front of Ryder so then it will be *Van*Ryder. Joy VanRyder. Doesn't that sound princess-like?"

I smile when I notice she's stopped talking.

We cut across the football field, and everything looks the same. Same goalie posts, same stadium seats, same green grass, tennis courts to the left, field house to the right. Maybe the school isn't as massive as I remember it. Maybe the bricks aren't quite as drab as I once thought. Or maybe it's just me that's changed.

"So what do *you* want to be?" she asks.

"A prince." I force out a laugh, and this pleases her, relaxes her a bit. She starts skipping way ahead of me, giggling to herself, showing off just another of her many self-conceited talents—a cartwheel. Only, her waitress skirt doesn't flip up the way cheerleaders' skirts do, so eager to reveal their tight, yellow panties. *Her* skirt sticks against her ample thighs and broad backside, and reveals nothing more than a pair of heavy, camel-brown nylons stretched over two chunky knees.

My gaze grazes from those knees to the field around us. One thing that definitely has not changed since high school is the fence that surrounds the property. One has to jump it to get into the forest. A fruitless deterrent the administration has designed to try and barricade high school students seeking schnapps and sex and a little light-up before or after class.

Despite the girl's cheerleading talents, she has a rough time making it over. Having straddled herself atop the metal fencing, she looks down at the distance she has to jump and hesitates. Once I'm over, I hold my hands out, as though to spot her, but instead she flips the other leg over and jumps down, pulling me forward until my hands are around her waist. And it feels so foreign to me—being this close and holding her this way. She's soft and smallish at the waist, between my fingers, just under my chin.

"Thanks." She giggles and takes a step back. And she really has no idea. Who I am. What I'm thinking. How much I want to hold her again.

We begin our way down the path. The same path I took with Melanie—just minutes before she declared she wanted to break up with me.

I feel a chill over my shoulders just thinking about it, just being back here. But now that I *am* here, I want to see the spot again. I need to.

"So how old are you?" she ventures.

"Eighteen," I lie.

"I don't really think age matters. Do you?"

Age has been everything to me. If I had been a year older, I may not have gotten out at twenty-one. Every month that passed, every birthday, every holiday, every mark of time, was a step farther through the bars. "No," I say. "Age is artificial. It's soulless. It doesn't matter one bit."

The forest seems much less enchanted than it had when I was fifteen years old. Much more guarded. Still, I know exactly where I am and exactly where I'm going. I lead the girl over rocks, between brush, and under tree limbs, lifting branches over our heads so they don't thwack her in the face, managing a scratch on my neck from one of them. I lick a spot on my sleeve and use it to dab at the blood, determined to keep moving.

We walk a bit farther until I find the spot—a clearing now littered with green and amber broken beer bottles. There's a cross jammed into the earth; fresh flower bouquets clustered around it; and old, weather-beaten copies of Emily Dickinson and Sylvia Plath, Melanie's favorite poets.

I walk closer and see a picture of Melanie, laminated, and sticking up like a fresh daisy. Her face, sweet and round and cheeky, like a cherub's, looking up at me—a time when she was still loving me. The picture is of her at her fifteenth birthday party. A wide birthday-cake smile across those cheeks, probably thinking how, in only a few hours, she would sneak out her bedroom window and meet me, *me*, who, per order of her parents, was not allowed to be at that party. And then how we would make love right here, on a blanket, under these stars. I think about those panties she wore. Pale pink with accordionlike strings that attached the front and back. A half-cup bra with ruffly pink shirring along the top. A bra that clasped in the front.

I wonder what type of underwear this girl has on.

"Robby?" she calls, a degree of concern in her voice. I wonder how long she's been trying to get my attention.

"Yes?"

"I think we should go someplace else. It's kind of creepy here. I've heard about this girl. Her boyfriend killed her. He beat her head in with a rock. Kids at school say she haunts these woods. They say sometimes you can see her carrying a rock around, seeking revenge on her boyfriend."

"What do you think about that?" I ask.

"Are you asking me if I believe in ghosts?"

"No. I'm asking what you think of some guy killing his girlfriend." I turn around to look at her, to catch her expression, but now everywhere I look is Melanie. Melanie's face. Melanie's smile. Melanie's eyes brimming with fear. Maybe this forest *is* haunted.

"I think maybe we should go," she says.

I'm able to blink Melanie away after several seconds. "Maybe it was an accident that she died." I approach the girl, put my hands around her waist like before and stare down into her eyes, do my best to fill them up with temporary confidence. "Maybe they just loved each other so much that their passion couldn't survive them both."

"Is that what *you* think?"

"Maybe. Maybe he still thinks about her all the time."

"Do you think about Kelly all the time?"

"Not right now." This eases the girl. I can see it in her

eyes. It's almost as though some thin, translucent layer of aversion, a layer not of her true self, breaks away, and what lies beneath is bright with innocence, like I could dive right in. I lead her away to a rock, and we sit down, facing one another.

"Do you think you guys'll break up?" she persists.

"I'm not sure she ever thought of us as together," I say, wondering if that in fact is the truth.

"I know what you mean. Remember that guy I told you about . . . my ex? Well, I guess maybe I thought there was more to the relationship than there really was. It's weird how we do that, you know, just fill in the blanks with our own answer key."

"I think we create our own reality, our own truths. If we believe it to be so, then it is so."

"I know what you mean. I really thought Jay and I— Jay's my ex—had something special, you know? Just the way you thought you and Kelly had something, too. And you know the worst part of it all? It was Jay and Joy. Even our names fit perfectly together. I mean, it's almost worth it to stay together for that reason."

I ignore her mindless rambling, her failing attempt at trying to compare some adolescent infatuation with what I have with Kelly. I say, "Why don't you tell me now what you said to Duggan?"

"Huh?"

"The guy in the diner."

"Oh, I just told him he should ask his princess to marry him once and for all. He's been dating her since he was fourteen years old. He's, like, thirty now."

I nod, taking in the word princess again, fully understanding now her childish longing to really be one. Almost endearing. I say, "Tell me it the way you told him. In my ear."

"Why?" She giggles.

"You'll see."

She leans forward and repeats the phrase into my shirt collar. She says it quick and loud and nervously, and then follows it with that schoolgirl giggle. "Okay?" she asks.

"No. I want you to say it slower."

"Why?"

"You'll see," I repeat, and nod my head like I'm the teacher and she should trust me. "Pretend that I'm the prince and this is the most important moment of your life. This is the most important thing you will ever say to anyone. It needs to be slow and quiet . . . and intimate, and you need to say it much closer to the ear."

She nods as though she understands, as though she wants to get it right. She leans in toward me and places her lips by my neck. Her breath is close to my ear. It's warm like dryer heat and I can smell the cherry candy from her mouth. She says softly, slowly, "I think you should marry your princess."

I close my eyes and imagine Kelly there, at my neck,

reciting one of her poems or telling me we'll be together soon and forever. I almost have to hold myself back from taking this girl, pressing her into my chest and holding her mouth at my ear for as long as I have strength or imagination.

When she draws her mouth away, I catch her glance with mine. Her eyes are wide and expectant, like endless tunnels of hope.

"Was that okay?" she asks, so close to my face I could kiss her.

"It was perfect."

"You're really handsome," she says. "People probably tell you that all the time, huh? Can I ask you a question that's going to sound a little dumb?"

I nod.

"Do you think I'm pretty? I know it's stupid and you don't have to answer. I just kind of wanted to know, you know?"

I stare down into those eyes—oddly large for such a tiny face, cinnamon-brown with bits of muddy black. Layer upon layer of gold-and-sparkling eye shadow—an attempt, perhaps, at making them appear smaller—only to make them look bigger. I stroke across her cheek, soiled with tan, Irish freckles, and teenage acne, and feel the layer of baby-hair fuzz beneath my fingers. A face that only a father could love.

I close my eyes and picture Kelly's face, her eyes, her

skin. "I think you're beautiful," I say, reaching behind her head and drawing her mouth closer, until our lips smear together. I wiggle my tongue through her lips and feel her mouth accept me. Her tongue folds over mine, and I feel myself reaching closer and closer inside her, my hands now kneading over the tops of her thighs, working their way under her dress, to see what panties she has on underneath—if they're pink and frilly and dip down low in the front.

"Wait," she says all of a sudden, plucking her mouth away, a loud and unpleasant suctioning sound. "What am I doing? I mean, I just met you."

I close my eyes and count to ten, try to remind myself of calmness. I say, "I really feel close to you right now. We can take this slow if that makes you more comfortable."

"What about Kelly? I mean, do you think you guys'll stay together? Because if you do, I wouldn't feel right."

I take a deep breath in and filter it out slowly, discreetly. I lean forward and kiss her lips once more, noticing for just a blink that her big red lipstick has smeared all over her mouth and chin, making it look like she's bleeding out the mouth. "I'm with *you* right now, okay? Remember that."

Melanie had been like this, too. Giving me excuses. Putting me off. Saying things that were irrelevant to the moment at hand. We never did get to make love that night. The night of her fifteenth birthday.

I close my eyes again, to picture Kelly harder, clearer,

but it's just Melanie again behind my eyes, in my head.

"Do you want to talk some more?" the girl asks.

"Of course I do," I say, and kiss her stronger, deeper, feel myself nearly biting her lip, suckling her tongue.

"Okay," she says, pulling away. "I'm an only child and my parents are divorced. They got a divorce when I was seven. It was kind of hard at first because I had to choose who to live with. So I chose both, you know, because I didn't mind traveling between the two of them. I'd live with my mother in the summer, then my dad during school, then back with Mom again for the holidays."

I nod and clench my teeth, counting up the number of freckles across her nose.

"Oh, and I also used to have a cat, Moses, but he died. Do you or did you ever have any animals?"

"No." Thirty-six freckles. One tiny pear-shaped birthmark beside her left nostril.

"How about your folks? Are they still together?"

I focus a moment on her neck, noticing how my hands would fit nicely around it, imagining my thumbs pressing in right below her windpipe. "Yes," I say finally.

"Do you have brothers or sisters?"

"An older brother," I say, still pondering, wondering how long she would put up a fight.

She smiles at me, apparently exhausted of her futile ramblings. I lean forward to kiss her again, noticing how her mouth is dry from all her trifling chatter. Still, I press myself into her, picture Kelly beneath me, and apply my weight to get her to lean back against the rock. My hand crawls up her thigh, finds the waistband of her panty hose, and begins to tug them downward. Her mouth pulls away and she takes a breath inward, as though to speak, to ask me another of her senseless questions, but I'm able to kiss it up and swallow it down just in time.

After a few moments, our kiss breaks and I catch my breath, working her panty hose down from soft, fleshy hips and buttocks. I can feel the panties now. I tug at them, feel the ample elastic, the cotton seams. The wrong kind.

"Robby?" she whispers into my ear. "What do you think of me?"

"Shut up," I bite, tugging up on her panties, getting them to wedge up into her thighs.

"Why?" she whines. "Why are you being like this? I really like you."

I pull back a moment, have to shake my head to get Melanie out. Like déjà vu. The girl is crying now, sobbing like the baby that she is; the baby that Melanie was.

"I'm sorry," I say after a giant breath. "I guess I just got carried away."

"Did I do something wrong? Because I really like you. I just want you to like me, too."

"I do," I snap, lamely trying to appeal to her incessant sense of insecurity. I take yet another deep breath in an effort to get a grip.

"A lot?" she asks, seemingly unaffected by my tone. "Like a girlfriend?"

"We'll discuss this later," I tell her.

She nods slightly and lays back, her head cocked to the left, toward the shrine—a faraway stare. I lean in and kiss her neck, try to bleed the image of Kelly into the moment, working my way up toward her mouth, still mauled with lipstick. Her stomach quivers beneath me, but when I look up at those eyes, that faraway stare, I see they're shrouded with resolve.

It makes me want to snap that stupid little neck of hers. "What's wrong with you?" I shout.

"I don't know. I thought maybe you might want to know something else about me. I mean, before we do . . . important stuff."

"Is there anything else you need to tell me?"

"How old was I when my parents divorced?"

"Why are you testing me?"

"How old?"

"Nine."

"No." She closes her eyes, I suppose to try and hide what she's feeling, the disappointment. "I was seven. Your parents are still together. You have one older brother, no pets, you don't think age matters, you like cheese omelets and sausage for breakfast, and you were away for five and a half years—maybe in military school."

I smile slightly, somewhat impressed, more so surprised.

I sit up, moving my weight completely off her. "I think you should go," I say.

"No," she says, startled. She jumps to a seated position and wipes at her eyes. "I don't want to go. I really like you. A lot. I just wanted to talk some more. But we don't have to talk if you don't want to. We don't have to say anything."

It's almost tempting. I reach into my pocket and offer her a napkin. It's the note for Kelly, but I give it to her anyway. The girl wipes at her eyes and blows her nose into it. "Just stay," she says.

I look over at Melanie's shrine and shake my head. "Maybe one day you'll realize what a lucky girl you are." I walk away, leaving her watery-eyed and red muddy-lipped. A dress rolled up around her hips. Torn panty hose pulled down to the tops of her thighs.

Just another lost princess.

Mearl Aremian

SATURDAY, AUGUST 12, 5:35 P.M.

On my to-do list of life, there are three things I have yet to accomplish:

1. Save someone's life.
2. Plant my roots somewhere and sprout a full garden.
3. Make lovecup with a boy who doesn't finish before I do.

I am determined to conquer at least one of these by the end of the day.

I'm standing in the lobby of the art theater at the

Peabody Museum, waiting for Ache to finally meet here with me as planned. I peer out the window toward the street, anticipating his arrival, but knowing somehow that he isn't going to make it.

My eyes stray up to the clock on the wall. He's already twenty-two minutes and seven seconds late. So why did he call me? Or, more important, why did I jump in response? Especially since I was already having a perfectly luminous time—losing myself in someone else's roots.

I look up at the movie board, noticing how it's blank. Just like me. Like the way I feel sometimes: a giant slate waiting to get filled, for someone to etch in all the missing parts—my history, my family, my genealogy. Why am I so drawn to the moon? Where did I get this jet-black hair, like a raven's wings? How come the tips of my upper eyelashes curl downward instead of upward?

I need to know these things.

I peek inside the theater, and it's empty, too. And so I just stare back at my reflection in the glass door, doing my best to make out any detail, checking that the two wooden wands that hold my hair in place are somewhat even, that there's a thick hennaed strand across my crown, like a halo waiting to happen. I rub under my eyes, noticing how some of my makeup has smudged, from my love-fest with Derik, I'm sure. I fish a tube of mascara from my bag and reapply, somewhat pleased by the look of the darkest eye makeup coupled with the palest lips, but still a bit disappointed—since my cheeks are filled with fallen milk-weeds instead of perennial roses.

I take a step away and glance back out the window, wondering where Ache is, if he intended on taking me to a show, or if it's *because* of the theater's emptiness that he wanted to meet me here.

Either way, I need to leave.

I make my way outside and inhale the warm, haunted air; the taste of sea and the promise of home. I'd give almost anything to be able to call someplace home—to plant my roots, grow a thorny bush of offspring and roses, and bathe under a fiery yellow sun forever and ever. I've been living here in Salem for the past year, the longest I've ever stayed anyplace, but I haven't actually rooted. Before here, I'd choose my many residences by their name. And so it was Mystic and Pleasure and Paradise and, before that, Clearview, Sunnydale, and Love Valley.

But then I met Brian.

Brian's this guy from the Find-Your-Family Web site. He informed me that my biological father and aunt (my father's sister) may have lived here growing up. I paid Brian fifty dollars, and in exchange he told me that my aunt passed away when she was fifteen years old, that the cause was a weak heart, and that he believes her body was buried in St. Mary's Cemetery.

But one year later, despite visits to city hall, fruitless hours spent setting time at the library conducting research, and frequent drop-ins at the cemetery office, I've failed to find out if any of these details are true. Because Brian won't tell me my aunt's name. Because I don't have the five hundred dollars it would take to buy my past outright.

And so, in the meantime, as I save up the required fee, it's been a ritual of mine—to visit the cemetery at least a couple times a week to see if I can feel something, get some vibe. But instead I've just been falling in love with headstones, with the idea that one of them might be a part of me.

I stroll down Hawthorne Boulevard to the bus stop, noticing how the air is multilayered today—chocolate-cake thick and Cinnabon warm—like I could eat it all up in a few long breaths. I hop on the 468 and choose a window seat—one that offers a view of the sky. It's actually the perfect time of day for a cemetery visit. The sun is starting to pinken and fall. I watch it over the trees in the distance; it looks so close, like I could reach out my window and pluck it out of the sky, poke a hole in the side, and squeeze all the orangey-pink liquid onto my skin to make me warm.

When the bus nears the cemetery, I ding the bell to inform the driver I want to get off, and begin my stroll along the pathway that leads to some of my favorite headstones. I've grown attached to this one woman. Her name was Carlene, and she passed on nine years ago when she was eighty-two. Her headstone is made from the most dazzling polished marble—a dark ruby color like the inside of a tea rose.

I close my eyes and conjure up the mental image that

I have of her. I imagine that she had soft white hands, like doves of peace, and a giant smile that made the corners of her eyes crinkle up. A smallish woman draped in long and velvety A-shaped dresses, with jade-stone jewelry, and a tiny voice with a tinkling little laugh. I've decided that she bore four children—three girls and a boy—and had eleven grandchildren. I imagine that they often gathered at her house for Sunday dinner after their family prayer practice, that they reminisced about family campfires under a waxing moon, and that her oldest son would often retreat to the back porch in search of shooting stars and fireflies, like his dad, Carlene's late husband used to do.

I gaze up toward the sky for the last quarter moon, fantasizing what it would be like to wane—to get smaller and duller each night until I just disappeared, until my tiniest speck of light went out. Only to start anew the following day. I know that most of what I've imagined about Carlene is true, that the light inside her was as big and full as a harvest moon; I know it like I know the sun will rise up again tomorrow.

I take the turn that leads to Carlene's row and, to my surprise, there's someone sitting on the bench by Carlene's grave. Some girl, maybe a couple years younger than me— sixteen or seventeen—with twisty dark hair that stops at her shoulders, and a metal lunch box that rests atop her lap.

My heart tumbles slightly inside my chest, just imagining that it might be one of Carlene's relatives, one of her grandchildren, maybe. There's an enchanting arrangement of orchids and lilies in front of Carlene's stone; I'm hoping that this girl has brought them. I smooth out the front of my skirt and move toward her, wondering if it might be Rosa, Carlene's granddaughter. Of course, I'm not sure if Rosa is indeed her name, but that's what I've imagined it to be. I've also imagined that she believes in faeries and gnomes and goes searching for them in the woods at night; that she recently got jilted by her boyfriend after he found someone more grounded, less flighty; and that she's not the most secure about her appearance—how skinny she is and how long and blanched her fingers are.

"Good afternoon," I say, when I get close enough.

The girl looks so sad with her valentine-red face. Instead of responding, she merely nods in my direction, staring down at her rusty lunch box, at the scratched up picture of Princess Diana staring up from the lid.

"How are you feeling today?" I ask.

She's wearing a pair of short denim overalls and a T-shirt with holes in it, and there's a thin cotton jacket draped over her shoulders.

"I'm fine," she says.

"But your aura has such a murky haze."

"Excuse me?"

Her arms are all scratched, like seams in her skin have come unstitched, revealing the dried-up blood lining underneath. "I read auras," I say, sitting down beside her on the bench. "Do you want me to tell you what I see in yours?"

She responds by scooting away from me, toward the end of the bench, drawing the jacket tightly around her.

"Are you afraid of what you might hear?" I ask her. "Of what your aura might reveal about you?"

But instead of answering, she gets up and wanders away.

Alone, I look toward Carlene's grave, thinking how I had planned on setting some time with her this evening. I wanted to tell her all about that Derik boy I met today, how he has such a luminous spirit but how he'll never know just how lucky he is.

But first I want to talk to this girl, to set time with her, to know why her aura has such a murky haze.

She's taken a seat on another bench farther ahead. I give her a few moments before approaching. "Are you a relative of Carlene?"

"Who?" She looks up at me finally; her eyes are like bloody red hearts—all troubled and teary.

"Carlene," I say, pointing back toward her headstone.

The girl shakes her head and focuses on her lunch box, tapping her fingers against poor Diana's scratched neck.

"Then why did you leave the flowers?"

She looks at me oddly, her lips twisting in confusion like she has no idea what I'm talking about. Then she gets up and walks away; there's just the sound of her rubber sandals flip-flopping as they smack against her heels.

I take a deep breath and return to Carlene's headstone

for my visit, but I can't stop thinking about that girl. About how grievous she looked. About those scratches on her arms. Or that bloody-red heart face.

I blow Carlene a kiss and then hurry toward the street to see if I can spot that girl. It isn't too difficult to find her; she's sitting at the bus stop, her knees hugged in toward her chest.

I reach into my pocket for bus fare, since I'll need to head back downtown anyway. The girl sees me approaching and releases a sigh.

"Hi," I say to her. "My name is Mearl. That's pearl with an M."

But she doesn't respond.

"I'm sorry if I invaded your space back there. It's just that I thought you were someone else."

She shrugs, pointing her knees away from me.

"Were you visiting someone?"

She clears her throat and shakes her head, making me wonder why she was there in the first place; if, like me, she goes seeking connectedness, fullness. Or maybe she feels even lonelier than I do.

"So are you just out enjoying the day?" I ask, in an effort to find my answer.

But in lieu of answering, she stands up from the bench and moves to the curb, gazing down the street in search of the bus. "What time do you have?" she asks, peering back at me. Her jacket is still draped over her shoulders. I wonder why she doesn't put it on to cover up those scratches. Or maybe she wants me to see them.

I peek up toward the sun; its pinky-orange glow sinks down between tree limbs. "It must be nearing six thirty."

She nods and chews at her bottom lip to study me a moment. "Do you have a cigarette?"

"A bubble-gum one," I say, reaching for my purse.

She gives me a spiteful look that makes me stop, that tells me she'd prefer to have the kind that contain tobacco, tar, and arsenic.

"You shouldn't smoke, you know," I say, almost wishing that I had a *real* cigarette—for her, anyway.

"I shouldn't do a lot of things."

"Like what?"

"Like talk to strangers." She turns away to gaze back down the street. There are scratches on her legs as well—thin red lines that run down her calves.

"Do you live around here?" I ask her.

She shrugs. "What do you care?"

"I care a lot."

She turns around to glare at me, and I look toward the scratches on her legs, hoping she understands what I'm saying. "I'm not into that, okay?" she says, her lips bunched up in disgust. "I like guys."

"I like guys, too," I say. "See, we already have something in common."

"You're a freak," she says, but she's almost smiling

when she says it, so it doesn't mar me one bit. It's good to see her almost smile after such a valentine-red face.

"Hey, if you like cemeteries, I know this really interesting one on Charter Street," I say. "It's from the 1600s. I could show it to you."

"No thanks."

"Well then, will you let me buy you a cup of herbal tea? It's the least I could do for invading your space before."

"I'm all set."

"Then how about a palm reading?"

"Excuse me?"

"In addition to reading auras, I also read palms. I work at one of the psychic shops downtown."

"You're a witch?"

I shake my head. "I don't believe in organized religion. Why limit body, mind, and spirit in just one way?"

"I think people like you are full of shit."

"I like to call myself 'in touch,'" I say, rising above her remark. "On par with the lessons of nature. There's just so much to learn in Life School, don't you think?"

"I think I know all I need to."

The Jell-O nearly plops out of my bowl at the passivity of her response, at the idea of living in a world where learning could ever cease. This girl needs me.

"Please," I continue. "Palmistry can be very illuminating." I hold my left hand, palm up, out to her. "See this straight line?"

She nods, venturing a couple steps closer to look.

"This is my headline. See how it's strong and unwavering? This says that I have to know and experience everything for myself."

"Like what?"

"Like, making lovecup with a boy. You know, getting a chance to actually experience the lovecup bliss before it's all over. I mean, don't get me wrong, the sex is sunny and all, and I *have* experienced lovecup bliss before, but it's usually when I'm alone, you know, solo."

"Maybe that's something you want to keep to yourself." She makes a peculiar face, scrunching up her nose, like I'm offending her in some way.

"Oh, sorry," I say. "Does my openness repel you?"

"Why do you talk like that?"

"Like what?"

"All fake and full of bullshit."

I look back down at my palm, choosing to be strong. I point toward my line of fate. "See this line?" I say. "See how it's solid but how there are breaks along the way? This says I'll make it through the kinks. I sometimes think that's true, but other times, I don't know. Sometimes I don't know how anyone can make it through anything when they have no sense of who they are with respect to where they came from. Do you know what I mean?"

She shakes her head.

"I want to be *from* someplace. Growing up, my father

was in this underground group devoted to the Rising Moon and its New Day Coming, so we ended up traveling all the time, not really rooting in any one place. It was good in one respect because it enabled me to see so many crimson places, you know . . . to experience so many of life's purples and pinks. But at the same time, just when I was getting used to a place, when I'd met some kindred spirits, we'd leave."

"So?"

"So I never really got to root anywhere. And now, I've been doing all this research, trying to connect with people in my family. I've discovered that I might actually have roots here in Salem."

"Roots?"

I nod and run my finger over the crystal point of my necklace, trying to visualize strength, like a hot-air balloon that swells bigger and bigger but never pops.

"What *is* that?" she asks, gazing at it, at its hypnotic shimmer, perhaps.

"It's my crystal," I explain. "My guide. It helps me stay balanced; helps me focus my energy where I need it most, so I never feel lost."

"Well, that's bullshit," she says. "Because according to you, you're *already* lost."

I shrug her venomous words away since she obviously doesn't understand—since she's obviously a great deal younger than me. "I've been trying to follow a lead on my roots," I say finally. "The problem is I don't even know my real name. The name on my birth certificate isn't my family name."

"Where's your dad now?"

I shrug again. "Underground somewhere. Probably in Mexico. That's where he was bound for, last I heard. About ten years ago, when I was nine, he dropped me off with the owner of a floral shop and never came back. I remember it was Valentine's Day. The shop was really busy, and I got to help out by poking these plastic heart sticks into the center of bouquets."

"Are you kidding?"

"About the plastic hearts?"

"About him just leaving you there."

"He only did it because he loved me, because he was becoming so immersed in that group and wanted me to have a crimson life, you know? Normal. But ever since, there's been a hole. Rust." I look toward the holes in her T-shirt.

"So, what if you can't find all that stuff out?"

"I have to. It's just always been a dream of mine, you know, a goal, to find my roots, to connect with them, to be *from* someplace. I've never been from anywhere."

"That's fucked," she says, running her fingers through that twisty dark hair.

"Why?"

She looks away. "Because I've lived here my whole life and never felt connected to anything."

I nod, having suspected that that was the way she felt. I peek down at her hands—a thick layer of olive skin; fingernails chewed down until the nubs are raw and bleeding; and knuckles the size of gum balls. And then at her arms— thin blood-filled scratches up to her elbows, like grappling through bushes, trying to find a way out. "Let me prove you wrong about palmistry," I tell her.

"And what'll I get?" she asks.

"What do you want?"

She nibbles at her lip to study me again—my face, my hair, the way I can't stop fussing with my crystal guide. She looks down at her lunch box and jiggles it back and forth, a tiny smile creeping across her lips. "You'll have to do what I tell you to, okay?" she says. "No matter how messed up it might seem to you."

"It isn't something illegal, is it?"

"Oh, no," she says, her smile growing by the moment. "Nothing like that." The bus pulls up, but she waves it away, taking a seat next to me on the bench. "We'll get the next one."

"Can I at least know your name?"

"Maria," she says.

"Maria." I smile. "It's superb to meet you. We're all cosmically destined in Life School, don't you think?"

"Whatever," she says, her face screwing up again. She slips on her jacket and opens her palm, inviting me to study it—the lines of her fate and life and love and spirituality.

"This line here," I say, "shows you'll live a long life. But see all these breaks? These show complications, you know? The rough stuff."

I glance down at her scratches, noticing how a couple of them are peeking out from the sleeve of her jacket. I want to ask her about them, but I'm afraid that if I do, she'll want to leave. Finally, she pulls the cuff downward to cover the scratches up.

"See this line in the middle?" I say, looking back at her palm. "That's your fate line."

"And what's my fate doing?"

"It's broken," I say. "See here, where your life line interrupts your fate line? That means that stuff goes on in your life that keeps you from reaching your destiny. And this line, here, your line of sun? This also interrupts your fate line."

"What does that mean?"

"Your line of sun speaks of your spirituality and well-being. But yours is weak, except where it breaks your fate. Your love line, too; it's crossed by branches of your fate and sun. Even your family line crosses your love line. It's like there are so many kinks, but your lines can't quite make it over them."

"I guess I don't have a chance," she says, but she's laughing when she says it, like she's long been resolved to a fruitless future. Like it comes as no surprise at all.

"Sure you do," I say. "There's always a chance in Life

School. It's all about learning. Just ask yourself, what in your life causes difficulty. What harnesses you from attaining your goals? If you can identify that, you can change your own fate."

"Easy," she says.

"It's not easy. In my case, my family line interrupts everything—my fate, my sun, my mind—though, at the same time, it's the dullest line of all. I just have to remind myself of that every once in a while so I don't let my lack of roots consume me." I inhale a cleansing breath, thinking how good it feels to be reminded.

"I don't know why you can't just plant your own roots," she says. "Why can't you just decide to be someplace and then be there? Make friends there? Make a life there? Why do you need to rely on people who obviously don't know or give a shit about you, to get on with your life?"

"Don't you believe in a sense of blood relation?"

"I have no reason to. And from what you're saying, neither do you."

Her verbal acid sinks into my chest, eats a hole in my heart, makes me want to cry bright fiery tears. But I don't. I can't. I have to be strong for her. Maybe she doesn't know what she's saying. Maybe she's just trying to be honest with me.

"Can I ask you just one question?" I say.

"What?"

"Does your family line interrupting your love line

have anything to do with these scratches on your arms?" I pull up on her sleeve, and finger over one of them, the blood still a bit fresh.

Maria responds by snatching her arm away. She stands up and grabs her lunch box—a scratchy-eyed Diana staring into my knee. "Fuck you!" she says.

"I just want to help you, Maria."

"Help *yourself*," she huffs. "You're so fake, pretending to be all sensitive and everything. You're not fooling anyone with all your sunny pink bullshit."

I feel my jaw tense, my chest weep. I sit up tall, trying to retain confidence, trying to assure myself that none of what she's saying is true.

"You're not even worth it to me," she says, glancing down at her lunch box. She turns on her heel and dashes down the street, leaving me alone.

I fold up from the bench, feeling completely defeated—filled with more rainy-day sadness than I thought I'd ever know. Still, I decide it would be best to go after her.

I begin walking down North Street. Maria actually isn't that much ahead. I follow as she takes a bunch more streets, keeping at least three shop lengths behind her as she continues on to Hawthorne Boulevard, passes the Irish church, the wig shop, and crosses the street to the bank. There's one of those old-fashioned phone booths in the parking lot, the novelty kind. I watch from the alcove of the wig shop as she steps inside the booth to make a phone call. The fusion of scents in the air—of oily hair mixed in sweet perfume—makes me feel queasy.

Four minutes flip forward on the digital bank clock. Then ten. I wonder what's keeping her. I cross the street and approach the booth. Her back is toward me, but she's not on the phone. Her head is down and she's curled up in the corner. I knock.

"I'm busy."

"Please, Maria," I say. "I want to speak with you. I want to help you. Don't you realize? We were fated to meet."

Since we're so much alike.

Maria turns to face me, her eyes all red and spider-veiny. I imagine her aura as a solid black cape over her shoulders. Her lunch box is wide open on the ground. Her sleeve is rolled up. And there's a safety pin, of all things, jammed deep into her inner forearm, all the way in.

I fold the door open, and there are blood tears running down her olive cheeks. "Here," I say, "let me help you." I take her arm and cradle it in mine, pull up on the safety pin and pluck it out.

Maria allows my arms to wrap around and hold her. I feel her fingers press against my back. And I think how it must have been destiny that Ache and I never did end up meeting today. How maybe Maria's the first real friend I've met since I got here.

How maybe I've accomplished a lot today.

Ginger Dubinsky

SATURDAY, AUGUST 12, 5:45 P.M.

I don't know Kelly Pickerel. But I know *of* her.

I know that Mr. Vargas, the computer teacher, paid her two hundred dollars to give him a blow job, and that she ended up doing it, right there in his classroom, right under his desk. That's what I heard. I also heard that she did it in the park with four guys from the lacrosse team—all four at once!

She's one of those girls who, on the surface, everybody *thinks* they want to be like—pretty, popular, lots of boyfriends. Except as soon as she opens her mouth you can tell she's really a bitch and a slut, and everyone knows it.

I flip through the scrapbook I've found at the back of

her closet. She's got some pretty screwed up hobbies. It's loaded with all these old newspaper clippings about some guy who murdered his girlfriend.

"Ginger?" Emily calls from the doorway. "What are you doing in Kelly's room?"

"Your mom asked me to clean," I say, draping one of Kelly's scarves around my neck—a purple shimmery one with silver threads woven throughout. "Go play."

Emily gives me a pouty face, but she knows better than to give me shit, so she just stomps off.

I love babysitting for the Pickerels. Not that I love kids. I *hate* kids. I hate all kids over six and under thirteen. My sister Sadie is eleven and she's the worst. Emily is five, so she's borderline.

Babysitting here is cool for the following reasons:

1. Mrs. Pickerel only goes out for two hours, tops.
2. She pays me fifteen dollars an hour, plus a big tip.
3. Emily doesn't mind playing by herself.
4. Unlike my mother, Mrs. Pickerel could probably care less that I'm a dancer. So she doesn't care when I pig out on her snacks. Doesn't say anything about how many Suzy Q's are gone from the package. Or how big my thighs are. Or how straight my back is when I do a pirouette.
5. Kelly's away in California for the summer, visiting her father, so her room is ripe for snooping.

164

Of course, it wasn't easy landing this gig. I had to work for it. I knew Kelly had a younger sister, and when I found out through Cheryl's older brother's friend Jessie that Kelly was going away for the summer, a lightbulb clicked on over my head.

The day after she left, I went by Kelly's house, rang the doorbell, and introduced myself to Mrs. Pickerel. I told her that I was fairly new to the area, just riding by on my bike, looking for kids (potential clients), noticed she had some (from the telltale swing set in the yard), and was wondering if she'd ever need someone to look after them once in a while. Then the clincher: I started talking about all my plans for college and how I was *already* saving up, how I was the freshman class treasurer at Salem High, certified in CPR, and a classical ballerina, happy to pass on my dancing skills to small children, namely hers. A perfect blend of responsibility, brains, *and* talent.

But I think what really did it was the résumé I typed up, with the carefully chosen font—Comic Sans—to show my fun, yet professional side. I listed my work experience in bold: a babysitting job of Cheryl's that I passed off as my own, a fund-raiser thing I'd organized (a chocolate sale I'd read about in some book for English class), and a volunteer summer gig at the Crombie Street Shelter. *All* completely bogus.

All so I could get into Kelly Pickerel's room and teach her a lesson once and for all.

Of course, I can't just rifle through her room *every* time I'm here. Emily would get suspicious and I'd be fired. I have to be discreet, rummage through in stages, cover one area at a time (like today, for example, with her closet). Plus, I'm not just looking for *anything*. I'm looking for *the* thing. The one ingredient that will really bring Kelly down.

A couple weeks ago I went through her bookcase. They say you can tell a lot about people from what they read. Plus, since I like to hide stuff in and between books, I thought this might be the most incriminating place. She's got a few copies of stuff I've read—Judy Blume, Christopher Pike, Maya Angelou. But mostly it's all these touchy, feel-good, self-help books. Titles like *When Nothing Matters Anymore*, *Fighting Invisible Tigers*, *Get Over It*, and *When Love Hurts*. Total snore material.

The time before that, I looked under her bed. I found one of those fire-safe boxes. At first I thought I'd hit the incriminating jackpot, seeing that there was a key sticking out of the lock, but instead it was kind of . . . weird. There was all this stuff crammed inside. One of those plastic snow globes with a family of yellow cats holding paws in a circle, one spotted cat in the center. A handful of foreign coins. A set of rosary beads and a laminated picture of the Virgin Mary. And then, at the bottom of everything, as if it were a liner, a folded up drawing of a whale. It had been done with little-kid hands, in crayons, and signed at the bottom: *Love Kelly*. At the top it said *To a Whale of a Dad*.

I could tell it'd been crumpled up, and that Kelly had done her best to try and straighten it out.

It made me wonder if my dad still kept my old art stuff. Or if it, too, ended up crumpled into a paper ball.

The closest I've ever come to actually talking to Kelly was this past year. I had my hair braided and then spiraled around the crown of my head. I don't normally wear it that way, but I was being dragged into Boston right after school to try out for the *Nutcracker* (my mother's stupid idea), and needed to have it up. Kelly and her friend, this girl Maria, were talking in the courtyard outside the school gym. Kelly tapped me on the shoulder as I walked by them. "Hey, freshman," she said, "do us a favor and be the ashtray." Then Maria, the smoking one, flicked her ashes in my hair, and Kelly let out this loud hyena laugh.

Then, one time after school, right before Thanksgiving, I saw her walking with some jock-guy from the lacrosse team. He had his arm dangling around her shoulders, but he kept moving it down to tickle her waist. She was laughing extra loud, like she wanted everyone to hear how much fun she was having—she thinks she's so great. But then she saw me, just standing there watching her, and her expression changed—two rock-hard eyes; one long, tight slit of a mouth—like she was mad or embarrassed or something. She peeled the slit open for only a second to mouth the words "go screw" at me.

But my worst run-in with the bitch was right at the

beginning of finals last year. It was in study hall, in the cafeteria, and I was talking to Matt, this guy in my algebra class who I'd been majorly crushing on for the past two quarters. Of course, Matt didn't know about my crushdom—at least I don't think he did—because I'd been pretending to be interested in his math skills (yeah, right!). Anyway, while the two of us were reviewing his Pythagorean theorem notes, Kelly and her bitch friends were sitting a full two tables back, but I could still hear their huge junior mouths. Obviously none of them cared about passing finals or getting into college or anything, because not even one of them had a book opened. I kept eyeballing Mr. Vargas the whole time, wanting him to say something to them. I mean, after all, it was *study hall*. But he just kept flipping through the pages of his newspaper like the overweight and underpaid slouch of a teacher that he is. Not that I ever really expected him to reprimand his precious Kelly; that could cost him some serious nookie points.

Anyway, after a good twenty minutes of listening to Kelly's hyena laugh, I felt something hit against the back of my head. I ignored it at first, hoping it was just a fluke, but then I felt more.

"Hungry?" I heard someone shout out.

At the same moment, a handful of sunflower seeds landed on the table in front of me. I looked up at Matt to see if he'd noticed. He had. He was staring right at Kelly and all her bitch friends.

first. I peel the paper back from the Scooter Pie, take a giant bite, and think up what I'm going to say to Sean. Maybe while I'm talking to him I could mention that his girlfriend has a twisted idea of what goes in a scrapbook. I flip it open and glance over the pictures. A closeup of a boy handcuffed and being led into a police car. A class picture of the girl he killed. She's got this giant crooked-teeth smile wedged up her face, like being killed by her boyfriend is the last thing she expects. Sucks for her. Then there's a picture of a rock, the murder weapon, with blood spatters on the point.

Perfect breakup ammo!

I swallow down the last bite of the Scooter Pie, press STAR-SIX-SEVEN to block the caller ID, and dial Sean's number. "Hello, is this Sean?" I ask when a boy picks up.

"Yeah. Who's this?"

"A friend."

"Tell me who this is or I'm gonna hang up."

"No you won't."

"Why won't I?"

"Because I know stuff that you'll want to know."

It's church-quiet on the other end, like maybe he's deciding. "Like what?" he finally says.

"Not so fast. Before we go any further, I want you to know that we may have seen each other before, but we've never actually spoken. In other words, there's no point in your trying to guess who I am."

"Why don't *you* just tell me who you are?"

"First answer my questions. You're Kelly Pickerel's boyfriend, right?"

"Yeah."

Yes!

"So, have you been a good boy while she's been away in California?"

"Who *is* this?"

"Is that a yes or a no?

"Who the hell is this?"

"Not quite the response a faithful boyfriend would give." The phone falls quiet again, but I'm feeling good about the way the conversation's going. I know I hold the winning hand, and I think he's starting to know it, too.

"Tell me what you're talking about or I'm going to hang up."

"I told you already, I know stuff. About you. About her. Do you want to know if Kelly's been a good girl?"

"I already know the answer to that."

I smile, hearing him fold. "Really?"

"Yeah."

"So you know about Robby, then."

"Who?"

And as soon as the name shoots out my mouth, I peek back at a scrapbook page, at the boy's name glaring from an article heading, and make the connection. *Robby Mardonia. So freaking good!*

"What do you think of murderers?" I ask.

"Murderers?"

"Yeah, you know, guys who off their girlfriends."

"What are you talking about?"

"We need to talk in person." I lean back against Kelly's puffy watermelon comforter and flip my legs in the air so that the skirt of the dress jumps up around my hips. Perfect dancing attire. "There's stuff I need to show you," I say. "Stuff you'll want to see."

"Either tell me over the phone or I'm hanging up now."

"I told you, Sean. There's stuff I know about *you* too, so don't even pretend you have a choice here." I flip over onto my belly and feel a shift beneath the comforter. It's another one of Kelly's feel-good books, *License to Cry.* I flip a couple pages, the corners folded over to bookmark her place—a chapter on isolation; stuff about dark days and even darker nights.

I mumble to Sean to meet me in an hour at the Dunkin' Donuts on Derby Street, hang up, and continue reading. But then my cell phone starts ringing. It's Cheryl. She wants to know how it's going, and so I tell her. She couldn't be more impressed; she just keeps screaming "Ohmygod! Ohmygod! Ohmygod!" into the phone.

There isn't anyone who wouldn't just *love* to see Kelly Pickerel go down.

But then, as soon as I tell Cheryl about our little field

trip to Double D's, she gets all nerdy on me, "I can't go out," she says. "My mom wants me to stay in tonight. She thinks I need to catch up on my summer reading."

"That's such bullshit," I say, tossing the book toward my bag.

"I'll try to sneak out and meet you there," she promises.

"Try hard," I say, and hang up. Sometimes Cheryl can be so lame.

I take a last peek at myself in the mirror, finally decide the dress is butt-ugly, and grab another—a short black spandex one that dips low in the front. Mega-slut material. I can just picture Kelly in it at some cheesy-ass club, dancing that stupid side-to-side-and-clap shuffle that people who have no rhythm resort to, having to yank the skirt part down every other second 'cause her fat ass rides it up.

I bet it would fit me just fine. I stuff it into my bag along with the *License to Cry* book and change back into my wet shorts and T-shirt.

Now what?

Mrs. Pickerel will probably be home in less than half an hour. I need to take advantage of every moment. I grab a couple Suzy Q's from the cupboard and stash them in my bag for later, along with two snack-size cans of potato stix. Then I scavenge my way through Kelly's closet a bit more.

She's got a bunch of cool shoes. Prada and Kenneth

Cole. I recognize a pair of black platform pumps in the corner. She wore them last Valentine's Day with a pair of navy blue kneesocks, a short plaid schoolgirl skirt, and a chest-hugging baby tee that showed off her gut. She thought she was *so* great. I pause a moment, wondering how that outfit would look on me, if I would look like just as much of a ho as her, or if it actually might be kind of cute. But then decide it would be way too warm for a day like today. There's a pair of creamy leather slingbacks that have my name all over them. They have a thick wedge heel and gold-lined strapping that winds around the ankle. They're a full size too big, but I fasten them on anyway and walk around the room. Not too bad, especially if I'm outside in this heat and my feet are swollen. I toss them in my bag and decide to browse around for a matching purse.

She's got about a hundred of them. They're on a shelf above the clothes. I go to pull a couple down, when I notice an old jewelry box sitting toward the back. I grab it, noticing how Kelly's name is imprinted on the top in sparkly gold cursive. I flip the latch, open the box up, and music starts playing—that "When You Wish Upon a Star" song from *Pinocchio* . . . the one Jiminy Cricket sings. There's a headless ballerina dancing in circles to the tune. I pick the head up from the bracelet compartment, noticing how she looks like a plastic version of Kelly—except the face and hair have been scribbled over with black Magic Marker.

There's a sticker pasted up over the faux diamond–

encrusted mirror at the back of the box. It's one of those pro-vegetarian don't-harm-the-animals ones—a frowning chicken holding a big fat drumstick. It says COWS HAVE FEELINGS, TOO. Below it, there's a poem written on the floor of the box in black marker:

Alone and glum
My world gone numb
Just want some love
Just want to rise above
But how can that be?
When there's no one but me
Ugly to the core
Don't want to deal anymore

I close the box back up and return it to the shelf, wondering how old Kelly was when she did all this. The whole idea of it weirds me out, like maybe I should clean up and go check on Emily.

Before tucking the scrapbook back in the closet, I flip it open, extract a short article from a page that looks pretty full without it, and jam it into the side pocket of my backpack. Then I head out into the family room. Emily's still got her nose pressed practically up against the TV screen.

"Hey, Emily," I say, sprawling out on the sofa, "wanna

of my backpack, wishing I had borrowed one of Kelly's designer totes. The touch of the article clipping helps to ease me a bit, helps to release the tight little knot I feel tied up in my chest. I'm able to let out a breath, remind myself that this is for fun, to pay Kelly back for being such a whoring little bitch.

Sean takes a seat at the table next to mine, and he's just . . . staring. He's sipping his coffee, but he's looking right at me. I lick the jelly globules off the nubs of my fingers and savor every moment, trying my best not to laugh out loud. Two more bites in, and I decide I might like another snack. I scoot out from the table and make my way across the floor, bending slightly over the counter, like I can't see all the doughnut selections from where I'm standing. "I'll have a jelly cruller," I say, hoping Sean's taking a good look.

I don't even bother with a bag this time. I tell the counter hag she can keep it, and instead lick at the tip of the cruller as I swing my hips pendulum-style back to the table. Sean's looking. He's watching the way my mouth fits around the doughnut stem, the way my ass sits just right in this dress.

I slide back into the seat, and Sean gets up, plunks himself down into the chair across from me at *my* table, and just keeps on staring.

"Hi," he says.

"Hi." He looks a bit different than he does in Kelly's winter ball picture—taller, thinner, a lot more tan.

"Do you have something to say to me?" he asks.

"No." I let out a nervous giggle and then bite down on the skin of my tongue to stifle the full-fledged laugh I feel pushing in my chest.

"I think you do," he says.

"Nope." I bite down fully on the cruller tip and smile at him as I chew it down.

He leans forward on his elbows and he's really kind of cute—soft brown eyes with dapples of tawny yellow; wavy brown hair painted over with golden sun streaks; modest muscle bulk.

Way too good for Kelly Pickerel.

I hold the cruller stem out to him. "Wanna bite?"

"Tell me what you gotta tell me," he says, "or I'm leaving."

"Well, aren't you a lousy sport?" I spoon up a globule of jelly with my finger and poke it into my mouth.

"I don't play games," he says.

"Not what I hear," I sing.

"Oh, yeah? What do you hear?"

"Stuff."

"What, is this fun for you?"

"Kind of." I giggle. "But I know a way we can have much *more* fun." I poke the now-four-inch cruller into my mouth and almost choke on some crumbs. I've stuck it in too far.

"How did you get my cell phone number?"

"Are you serious?" I ask between coughs. "That was *so* easy." My eyes are watering now. I take a sip of my Coolatta to ease the tickle in my throat, but almost end up spitting it all out. It's *way* too bitter.

"So what do you have to tell me about Kelly?"

"Wouldn't you rather talk about something more interesting?" I lean in closer and imagine venturing my fingers across his forearm. "Like, what we'll be doing later?"

He yanks his arm away. "I'm not doing anything with you."

"Why not? Don't you like girls?" I poke my finger into the jelly filling and suck at the tip.

"I'm outta here," he says.

"Okay, fine. I'll tell you." I rip open a sugar packet, add it into my Coolatta, and stir it all up with a straw. "So I know some stuff about Kelly."

"Like what?"

"Like, that she's cheating on you with another guy, some murderer from California." Proof positive that she's a backstabbing bitch. I take another sip of the Coolatta and add two more packets of sugar.

"How do you know that?"

I end up showing him the article clipping and telling him all about the scrapbook at the back of her closet. I tell him about the girl who called, the diner, and how Kelly left her cell phone there this morning. I even throw in the rumors I've heard about her—blowing Mr. Vargas and her gang bang with the guys on the lacrosse team. And at the end of all of it, instead of being ripshit like any other normal guy, Sean wants to know what I have on *him*, what I meant when I said he didn't seem faithful.

And suddenly, I think, Holy shit, this guy's been scamming, too.

"I guess I heard you've been cheating on Kelly," I say, flipping my hair back the way Kelly did in the courtyard that day; leaning back in the seat so he can admire the dress, how it looks *so* much better on me.

"How? From who? Who told you that?"

So completely pathetic. "You know what?" I say. "I gotta go. You're way too lame-ass to be seen with me. No wonder Kelly's cheating on you." I frown at another sip of my Coolatta. "I have a *real* man to see tonight."

"Not until you tell me who you heard that from."

I look over at the crusty guy, still reading his funny papers, and say, "My papergirl told me, all right?"

"Your papergirl?"

"Yeah, I don't know, she said she was delivering the papers and saw you in action. I don't know *how.*"

At that, Sean dissolves into a slushy, dirty mass, like I could flush him down with the push of a finger. I almost feel bad for him. Except my cell phone is ringing and I have to answer it. "This is probably one of my boyfriends now," I say, plucking the phone from my bag, suspecting that it's really my mother, that she's going to be pissed I haven't come home yet—since she's already misplaced one daughter today.

But it isn't my mother. It's my pain-in-the-booty sister Sadie. Apparently some cop picked her up en route to escape and my mother's cell phone is out of range and Dad's working and can't be reached (even though it's Saturday) and there's some social worker there asking Sadie about her red and puffy eyelid and the No Feeding sign Mom pinned to her shirt.

I tell her I'll be right there and hang up.

"Sorry, Sean," I say, scooting out of the chair. "It's been fun, but I really gotta go. My man's waiting for me."

"Just tell me one thing," he says.

"What?"

"Why?"

"Why what?"

"Why did you call me? Why did you tell me all this? What do you want?"

"What do you mean?"

"I mean, you must have some reason." He's glaring at me like this is *my* fault, not hers, like it's my fault Kelly's such a lying, backstabbing ho.

"I don't know," I snort. "Because Kelly's, you know, kind of a bitch. Everyone knows it."

"You don't know her."

"I know *of* her," I say, "and that's enough for me."

"You don't know anything about her."

"Yes I do," I say, feeling a wad of tension cram itself in my jaw. "I know plenty."

"Yeah, like what?"

And then I think about it. About her room and what I found. That she used to pray to Mother Mary. But now Mother Mary is all closed up in a box.

I know about the spotted cat and the foreign coins, and that she probably misses her dad. Probably looks in books to try and find what's missing. But no words on love or hurt or isolation have ever helped bring Mary back.

I look away when I feel my eyes betray me and start to fill with tears. "Maybe you're right," I say finally. "Maybe I don't know anything. Maybe it's just me who's the bitch." I throw my backpack over my shoulder and pitch my Coolatta in the trash, now way too sweet from all that sugar.

Joy Ryder

SATURDAY, AUGUST 12, 2:55 P.M. WEST COAST TIME, 5:55 P.M. EAST COAST TIME

I have a rubber dick and I'm not afraid to use it. It used to belong to my mother. When I was little, she'd keep it in the night table beside her bed. I'd take it out and play with it, pretend it was a jumbo hot dog and that I was fixing a barbecue. Then I'd click it on and it would start buzzing and I'd pretend the noise was the sizzle of juicy meat, fighting to burst from inside the tight, hot dog skin, over pretend-flame heat.

Once I put a blob of brown yarn on it for hair and pretended it was Barbie's boyfriend, Buzz. Then another

187

time I poked it inside my underwear to see if I could make it look all bulgy, like a boy. But it was too big to squish the whole thing inside, and so it stood up straight, at least four inches of thick rubber dick pointing out the hem of my Cinderella panties like it wanted to chat.

Of course, I was only trying to get a rise out of my mother. Obviously I knew what it was. I'd seen the dangling wee-wees of the neighborhood boys, the Guerino twins, skinny-dipping in their pool, inviting me to come over and play Marco Polo, telling me to shut my eyes and reach out my hand for something long and wet.

My mom would take the rubber dick from me and hide it, but that just made me want to seek it out all the more. I'd find it crammed under a stack of bed pillows, sticking up out of an old coat pocket in her closet, or at the way, *way* back of her underwear drawer. I'd click it on and twirl it around and around, feeling its power sparkle through my hand. I'd be the princess, and the rubber dick, my very own magical wand.

You'd think that would have really put my mother over the edge. It didn't. She just got exhausted trying to hide it from me all the time, and so she finally let me keep it and got herself another. A bigger one. With a louder buzz.

I hold the rubber dick in my hand, gooey at the tip from old sticker jizz. A gash in the balls from the time I took it on a bike ride. I went over a bump; it jumped from my basket, fell to the ground, and I ended up running it over.

I've decided I'm going to put it to some good use once and for all.

I hate boys today. I hate the way they pretend that they like you when they smile and nod at what you're saying, like what you're saying is actually interesting to them, but then you ask a question or make some comment and realize they're not even listening at all. I hate it when they bring you into the woods because it's secluded and supposedly romantic and lean you back against a jagged rock that cuts right into your shoulder blade and makes you bleed.

When they make you breathe into their ear because it gets them all hot. And then stick their big, fat tongue in your mouth and waggle it back and forth. When they squish your boobs like it's fifth grade all over again, like boob-squishing is at all pleasurable for you. And go up your skirt and wedge your panties up the crack. And then leave, in the middle of everything, after you've told them about yourself and your family, that your parents got a divorce when you were seven, that your cat, Moses, died on your ninth birthday, and that you've always wanted to be a princess—like you're a stupid, *stupid* piece of dung.

I *hate* Robby. *Hate* him. I pick up the cell phone his girlfriend left at the diner today and start searching through the address list. I want to tell her what a backstabbing, two-timing slimeball she has for a boyfriend. I click on the number labeled HOME, talk to some girl who tells me Kelly's away for the summer, visiting her father. Hang up. Find the number labeled DAD. Bingo.

"Is Kelly there?" I ask.

"Just a second," some lady says.

"Hello?"

"Hi, Kelly?"

"Yeah."

"My name is Joy. Maybe you remember me? I'm the waitress from the diner you and Robby met at this morning. First, you left your cell phone at my station and now I have it. Second, and much more important, I wanted to let you know that your boyfriend is a two-timing piss puddle. After you left him at breakfast, he had me for lunch. And if he even tries to deny it, tell him it was in the woods, behind the high school, and that his wiener is the size of a Planters peanut. Toodles."

I hang up. That felt good, but not nearly good enough. I want to see for myself that he pays. I search through the phone's address list a bit more, hoping to find his number. I want to tell him what I did. I want to hear the pain in his voice when I fib and say that his girlfriend was crying when I told her. When I say that I told her that we PB-and-Jammed, even though we didn't, even though he ran off and left me spread-eagled in the middle of the woods. Left me alone there after I was almost ready to do it with him, after I told him all about myself. But his number isn't even listed in here, and I don't know his last name, so I can't exactly look him up. I click the phone off so Kelly can't call back, and toss it to the floor. *Double damn!*

But that's fine. I breathe. That's okay. Because I've still got my rubber dick. And there are still plenty of other boys to pay back while I figure out what to do about Robby.

First on my list . . . Danny Winslow. I *hate* Danny Winslow. More than anything. More than Robby from this afternoon, or Jay from last year. More than the skinny-dipping Guerino twins from the pool. Or peeping Mr. Gallo from next door.

And it's time I make Danny pay. Make them all pay—one by one. See how they like it . . . their lives being ruined by a stupid, ugly, pulsating dick.

Danny Winslow has made my life a living hell for five years, ever since the fifth grade. A whole year of bra-snapping and boob-pinching. Then two years of riding the bus with him, waiting at the stop while he called me names like Joy-the-boy and Rider-for-hire, and pulled at my hair, and hacked loogies into my lap. Then eighth grade, and all the prank phone calls to my house. All the heavy breathing and telling me how he was whacking off to the sound of my voice.

This past year was the worst.

We ended up in the same freshman algebra class. On the first day, he walked in, smiled when he saw me, and slithered into the chair next to mine. He'd make it a habit to come to class early and scoot the chair over extra, *extra* close. He'd lean into my ear and whisper something gross, *always* with peanut butter–flavored breath. "How about we slip into the janitor's closet?" he'd say. "I can lift up that skirt of yours and pull down those tights. And show you my dick and jam it right in. Doesn't that sound so nice? From behind? Right after algebra? You know you wanna, Joy Ryder. You know you wanna ride me."

And then algebra would start and I'd ask Mrs. Fitzpatrick to move my seat, because whenever she'd turn her back to write something on the board, Danny would ask me who I was sucking on that morning because my breath smelled like penis. But it only smelled that way because I was too nervous to eat and so my mouth was all dry and pasty. Nervous because of him. And what he'd do.

Mrs. Fitzpatrick would ask me why I wanted to move and I'd tell her because Danny was bothering me, but she'd just tell him to stop, to keep his hands to himself, to pay attention to what was on the board. At first I thought it was because she didn't want to mess up her seating chart, all those square tags of cardboard arranged in neat little rows; but then I realized it was because she just didn't believe me. Of course, it didn't help things when she saw me hit him. It was more of a push, really, to the shoulder, like that even hurts. But from then on she didn't take me seriously and told us both to grow up.

He would whisper my full name over and over again, inserting the words "I wanna" in the middle, telling me how much he wanted to screw me—and no one even cared. Most of the kids were lemmings and thought it was the funniest thing in the world to see me suffer like that. The few left over were either too scared of him, or just happy it wasn't them he was bugging, to bother sticking up for me.

I've stopped speaking to my parents several times for naming me after my father's motorcycle. My dad bought the Harley three years before I was born and dubbed it right away. Joy Ryder. The letters in flaming yellow with red sparks airbrushed to the sides of the gas tank. When I came along, he saw naming me after it as paying some tribute to his two most prized possessions.

I grab the rubber dick, along with all the money out of my piggy bank and a fistful of dollar bills from my shift this morning, and storm out of my house.

Danny Winslow lives just two blocks down. He and some other jerky boys play basketball in Danny's driveway every day after summer pre-season football practice. I've seen their routine. They come home from McD's, toss their hamburger wrappers into the trash, dump their bags on the porch, and hit the court.

Today, I'm going to crash the game. Cause a big stir. Flash them my loot and hope they let me join the game.

I'll just need to figure out which bag is Danny's. And I hope forty-one dollars is enough.

I can hear them in the distance. The ball bouncing, echoing against the pavement. When Danny sees me approaching, everything stops—my feet, my nerve, the plane flying above, even the echo of the ball—but then his voice breaks the air.

"Hey, Penis Breath, your stench is funkin' up the game."

Jeremy Hicks, the boy I used to play house with in the third grade, is standing behind him, the tips of his fingers tucked into his pockets.

I reach into my bag to feel the rubber dick, to feel its power and all it promises.

"Whatcha got in there?" Danny asks. "Some mouth-wash? You could use it."

"I've got some money," I say, fanning out a few ones.

"Why don't you take it and get your face fixed? You and Hicks can go together. Hey, Hicks." He turns to Jeremy. "Maybe you and Penis Breath can hook up and go to the plastic surgeon . . . get a group discount."

I hate my face. All the purply freckles jumbled over my nose and cheeks. My curly orange hair. Sometimes I feel like it's a costume, that I don't really look this bad. That my skin isn't really as chalky as I think it is; that my eyes aren't quite as big and buggy. That I'm not really this short. And my lips aren't so thin.

Jeremy laughs off Danny's comment, but I can't imagine he thinks all those oozy pimples are really funny.

I swallow down the fear I feel creeping into my mouth, poking at my eyes. "I want to use my money to play."

"What are you talking about?" Danny takes a couple steps toward me, and now we're just a few feet apart—his bullet-gray eyes aiming down at me; his curly brown hair in a sweat wad on his head; those stupid, furry eyebrows, like giant black caterpillars, across the center of his forehead. How I would just love to tell him how stupid they look.

I hate him. I *hate* him. I HATE him.

"I'll bet you twenty dollars that I can kick your caboose at PIG," I say, stuffing the dollars in my pocket.

"Are you serious?" he asks.

"Do you even *have* twenty dollars?" I ask.

His four clone friends start squealing in the background like the pigs they really are. Like this is the most action they've gotten in a long time.

"Yeah, I got twenty bucks."

"So you wanna play me?"

I suck at basketball; all sports, really. When I was little, I couldn't even play jump rope right, kept getting my feet all tangled up. But I don't care about winning this game, nor do I care about the twenty bucks. I know I'll win in the end, and that's worth all the money I have.

He socks the basketball into my gut and says, "You just made a big mistake, Penis Breath."

I dribble as best I can, both hands slapping at the ball, over to the net. "I wanna see your twenty bucks before we play."

Danny jogs, I'm-so-tough style, over to the bag-littered porch. He reaches into his bag, a nylon green one with white straps, extracts a wallet and approaches me, waving a twenty dollar bill in the air. "It's just you and me now, Penis Breath," he says, poking his finger into my chest, grinding it in hard to leave his mark.

"I don't mind," I say, my eyes still locked on his bag. "I've always wanted to play *you*."

"Yeah, well, you're really gonna get yourself fucked today."

"No shit," one of the lemmings chimes in.

"Sounds like fun," I fake giggle.

"Yeah?" Danny grabs his crotch. "All five of us on you?"

"No thanks," sweat-faced Bobby Eskinas yells. "Even I'm not that hard up."

"Oh, yeah, that's right," Danny says to him. "I almost forgot you prefer schlong."

I cock my head to the side and smile like what they're saying isn't what I'm really hearing, like we speak two different languages. And try my best not to cry or throw up.

I place my bag down on the porch, next to Danny's,

look over my shoulder, and they're all just standing there waiting for me. *Double damn!*

We start playing, and it's really no puzzle as to who's gonna win. Danny's first shot ends up a swish, and within five minutes I already have a big fat P. The lemmings are cheering him on at the sidelines and Danny's trying to act extra cool, getting all fancy, doing backward shots and under-one-leg tosses like he's so great. If I wasted every day of my life throwing a rubber ball at a stupid net, I could do that, too.

Two minutes later I have P-I.

"I smell pig!" Jeremy shouts out. I turn and look at him, can almost hear him—eight years old, whispering from inside the shed behind my house, *I'll be the husband and you be the wife and this will be our bedroom.*

"Yeah, Penis Breath, close your legs." Danny tosses the ball at my head to knock me back to earth.

At that, they all start laughing, Jeremy flopping back on the grass like it's the funniest thing he's ever seen and heard. My mouth starts trembling and I want more than anything else to cry—to be at home, in my room, under the covers, my nose pressed into my pillow in blubbering bliss. I look away to try and stop the emotion I feel building up on my face, to try and imagine myself floating above this whole scene, looking down on Danny and his pathetic friends and seeing them for what they really are— pure American white trash.

"Time out," I say, moving over to the steps. "I need a tissue." I hold underneath my nose, pretend that it's running.

"Aw, baby's crying," Danny says. He joins them on the sidelines and they all high-five one another.

Meanwhile, I fish into my bag for a tissue, making sure the rubber dick is well within eyeshot beside my change purse, and peek over my shoulder.

They're all just staring at me.

"I need to take a little break," I say, rubbing at my stomach and taking a seat on the steps. "I'm not feeling so good. Female stuff."

"Like we needed to know that," Danny says, poking his finger in his mouth like he's going to heave. "Two minutes or you're a big fat pig by default and I'm twenty bucks richer."

"She's a big fat pig anyway," Jeremy hollers.

They all start laughing again but then resume playing like I don't even exist. My bag still open, I can see the rubber dick from here. Danny's bag is just inches away. I decide it would be best to get his bag unzipped first and then make the transfer.

I place my bag atop Danny's, pretending to be searching around for something, using his bag as a makeshift table. While my left hand fishes around in my main compartment, my right hand, concealed by my bag, tugs ever so slowly at his zipper. I get it opened just a couple inches.

That's when I hear him—when my heart clenches into a rock-hard fist.

"Hey, Penis Breath," he shouts, glaring right at me. "What do you think you're doing?"

My mouth trembles open. My upper lip twitches.

"Get your infected shit off my stuff," he says, referring to my bag.

"I was just looking for something," I say, feeling my cheeks get extra hot.

"Off—now!" he demands.

My heart is moshing around inside my chest. I move my bag to my lap. Luckily, Danny doesn't notice that his zipper is undone a bit.

"Hurry up. I want my twenty bucks and then I want you and your ass-breath out of here." He turns his back. Jeremy, Bobby, and them are playing close to the net. In one quick motion, I grab my rubber dick and stuff it into Danny's bag so that the head sticks out from the zipper part.

"All better," I call out, giving my stomach a convincing pat—if I do say so myself.

We resume our game, I get the final G, Danny starts dancing around the driveway, demanding his twenty bucks, and I've almost won.

I pull the twenty dollars out of my pocket and hand it over. Danny starts counting up all the ones, practically my whole day's tip money, and then tells me to leave.

"I don't want to go just yet," I say. "Doesn't anyone else want to play me?"

"I got twenty," Jeremy yells out.

"I need to see it first," I say.

Jeremy walks toward the porch to fetch his moola, and I peek at Danny. He doesn't look happy with this arrangement. "I just wanna see if I can win my money back," I tell him.

"Only one way you're gonna win your money back, Penis Breath." Danny grabs his crotch and starts walking toward me.

"What do you mean?" I giggle.

"You know what I mean." He takes a step closer; his chest, shoulders, and head towering over me, making me feel two inches tall. And if I didn't believe in guardian angels before, I do now, because all of a sudden I hear Jeremy yell out, "What the fuck?" and I'm saved. Danny turns around, and Jeremy's pointing at the rubber dick, Barbie's former boyfriend, standing straight out the top of Danny's bag.

The other lemmings gather around. "What the fuck is that?" Bobby shouts. And then they start laughing and pushing each other and high-fiving, like this is the juiciest.

Danny storms over and rips the dick out of the bag. He's just holding it in his hand, and all the lemmings scatter like it's a bomb.

"Who put this in here?" Danny takes a step toward

them, the rubber dick now soaring in his hand.

"Hey, you keep the fuck away from me with that, man," Bobby says.

"No shit," Jeremy says. "Don't go gettin' any ideas. When you said you wanted to play ball, I didn't think you meant it like that."

"It's not fuckin' mine," Danny says. "You were the one who was over here."

"Hey, I was just gettin' my money."

Danny throws the rubber dick at Jeremy, but they're still all laughing like they don't believe him, like they're just as happy as I am that this happened. Danny turns to me and says, "Ha-ha. Is this yours? Did you put this in here, you bitch? Is this your fuckin' dildo, you fuckin' dyke?"

"Shut up, pretty boy," I say. "Why don't you run along now to the beauty parlor so you can get those furry eyebrows waxed?"

"Hey, it came out of *your* bag, man," Jeremy interrupts.

"Fuck you," Danny says to him. "Why don't you get the hell out of here, pansy."

"Hey, I'm not the one with the joystick in my bag."

At that, Danny lunges at Jeremy, grabs him around the T-shirt collar, and starts shaking him. "I said get the fuck out of here," Danny says, foam spitting out of his mouth.

Bobby and the other lemmings pull Danny off, and now it's just him against all of them, and me on the sidelines.

"Hey, this is my house," Danny says. "I want Jeremy out of here."

"How 'bout we all get out of here?" Bobby moves to the porch to grab his gear. "I'm nobody's bitch."

"No shit." Jeremy grabs his bag and swings it over his shoulder, and the other lemmings follow suit.

"Assholes." Danny furrows those furry caterpillar eyebrows and pushes by the group, grabbing his bag, storming inside the house and slamming the door, like he's gonna cry.

I walk home, feeling better than I have in a long time. In my room, I open up all the windows and invite the smell of fresh lilacs inside. Everything feels tingly and new. Fixed. Like a wound that's been healed, a tear that's been stitched.

I look in the mirror at the new me. My hair looks pretty today, the ends curling up like jelly rolls. My heart-shaped face with its pinkish glow. Pretty. Like a princess. A princess way too good for Robby from the diner, or disgusting furry-eyebrowed Danny Winslow, or any of the rest of them.

I twirl myself around and around, thinking about everything. About how good I look today. About what Danny Winslow must be doing right now, how he must be feeling. About making that phone call to Robby's girlfriend and how she'll probably break up with him over it. "I hate you, Robby!" I shout. "And you, too, furry-eyebrowed Danny Winslow. And all the rest of the jerky boys in this town. I hate all of you!"

But then I almost trip over my own feet and have to catch myself against the dresser. I look up and I'm caught in the mirror, and my reflection is just . . . staring at me, like the big liar that it is. A liar because, when I look closer, I see that I'm still wearing the same old costume. The same old freckly face. The same curly, ugly, carrottop-orange hair. Chubby, ruddy cheeks. Big, buggy eyes. And flat, colorless lips that blend right into my skin.

Princesses aren't supposed to be ugly.

I turn around to go into my bag for lipstick and eye shadow, but the bag isn't there. Isn't on my bed or slouched on the floor. Isn't in the kitchen or hanging in the mud-room. Isn't anywhere I can think of but one place: Danny Winslow's porch.

Double damn!

I eat up all the courage I can find in the pint-size container of Ben & Jerry's, and when I'm finished, start my walk over there. I'm hoping Danny hasn't dared come out of the house yet, that my stuff is still sitting on the bottom step, and that none of the lemmings did anything to it. I can just imagine them opening it up, finding my old Barbie doll (I put her in there so she and Buzz could have a chance to say their good-byes), a half-eaten olive loaf sandwich, my collection of glittery plastic sandwich swords (I carry them around for luck), and all my Bonne Bell makeup. My mind blows out a daydream bubble in which Jeremy Hicks and Bobby Eskinas wrap a Bonne Bell–made-over Barbie with a slimy piece of olive-spotted bologna and poke her with swords. I pop the bubble out of my mind and quicken my pace. Hurry past the Fourniers' boob-shaped bushes, across Broad Street, and two driveways down from the house still draped in Christmas lights.

And when I get there, all I find is an empty porch. No bag. No Danny. No lemmings. Nothing.

Triple and quadruple damn!

The house looks so empty, I'm thinking nobody's home, but when I walk up to the door, I see it's open. I press my nose against the screen to look into the kitchen and see if my bag is in there somewhere. There's a box of Nutter Butter cookies on the counter. I wonder if that's where Danny gets his yucky peanut-butter breath. If he's the one who left them out.

I don't see my bag anywhere, so I decide to knock. If Danny Winslow *is* home, I'll just stand up to him. I'll picture him the way he looked earlier: the rubber dick sitting in his palm; the recipient of all that lemming laughter; the ugly, disgusting, furry-eyebrowed worm that I hook-line-and-sinkered.

Except no one comes to the door.

I knock a little louder. And then LOUDER. But still nothing.

Assuming no one's home, I'm feeling somewhat

relieved. But I still need to get my bag. I'll bet Danny took it up to his room to see if I had any more money in there.

I open the screen door and tiptoe across the linoleum bricks. I've never just come into anyone's house like this before, and it's making me feel all jittery inside. What if his parents come home and find me searching through his room for my bag, thinking I'm some burglar? What if a neighbor saw me just walk in and has already called the cops?

What if Danny really *is* home? What if he knew all along I was outside and was just waiting for me to break in so that he can justifiably attack me for breaking and entering?

I make my way up the stairs, where I'm thinking the bedrooms are. My nerves are completely scrambled, fried up and ready for toast. But the house is so still—so quiet, like even if someone *is* home, they'd have to be sleeping or dead or in a coma or something. I tell myself this over and over again up each step to help ease the jitters.

There are three bedrooms at the top of the stairs. From where I'm standing I can almost see into two of them. One has a giant four-poster bed, so I'm thinking that it's his parents'. The other is decorated in princess pinks.

Danny's must be the one at the end of the hall. The one with the closed door. My heart is literally pounding out my chest, like I could almost grab it up in a beat. I think I'm going to be sick. I look to my left and see there's a bathroom there. I consider using it, throwing up all the scrambling inside. But I just need to get this over with.

I suck in a deep breath and throw the door open. Empty. There are clothes strewn all over the floor, empty food containers on the desk, football gear in the corner, Xbox stuff set up in front of the TV, but no Danny.

No Danny!

I let out a happy breath, pat over my chest to tame the wild beat, and start looking around for my bag. I see it right away, lying sprawled open on the floor, next to his bed.

My eyes wander up to the pillow. On it are Barbie and Buzz. Barbie's legs are wound around his hips and she's planting a big, sloppy kiss right on his face. I grab the bag and shove them both inside. Then I check the side pocket for my remaining money. Oddly enough, it's still there. Only my makeup bag isn't.

I start looking around the night table for it, even check inside some of the drawers. No luck. I move over to the dresser and peek up into the mirror. But instead of seeing myself, I see Danny.

He's standing behind me in the doorway—a football jersey down to his knees, tube socks up around his calves, my cherry-red lipstick across his lips, the vee at the top accentuated by flawless application, like he's been wearing it all his life.

I feel my mouth drop open because I can't believe it, and I don't think he can either, because he's staring at me like he's just as shocked. I turn around for a better look at him and see that one of his eyebrows looks different. Less furry. Plucked into a princess-worthy comma. And I'm pretty sure it's bleeding, too.

The whole scene makes me feel sad. Sad because of the rubber dick, because of how unhappy he looks, and because I was the one who made the furry-eyebrow comment.

Me and Danny just stand there and stare at each other, and all I can think is at least it's a happy ending for Barbie and Buzz, who have once again found each other.

Sean O'Connell

SATURDAY, AUGUST 12, 9:30 P.M.

I never really thought of Nicole Bouchard as being much more than some girl I grew up with. The quiet, Brillo-haired skinny girl who always looked the same, whether it was the second or the tenth grade. Who never grew boobs and always wore braces, and always did her homework, even for art class.

The girl I could never hate because she was the one who got me through geometry, who slid her quizzes to the edge of the desk so I could copy down all those formulas for pis and squares. The girl I knew kind of had a crush on me, because I'd constantly catch her watching me—on the field, during class, from behind her locker. Because she'd come to all my hockey games. And include me on her Christmas and Valentine card list—the envelopes sealed with smelly fruit stickers—even though we never shared conversations much longer than "hi" and "what's up?"

The same girl who had her best friend call me up to ask if I'd go to the Sadie Hawkins dance with her last fall, who listened in on the other end of the line to see what I'd say—like it was fifth grade all over again and she was too afraid to call me herself.

That girl. The one whose best friend I ended up asking out.

And yet . . . it was just earlier today that I was rolling around naked with her in her mother's flower garden. When I noticed that she wasn't wearing those braces anymore. And her body didn't look quite so skinny. And the Brillo-pad hair had gotten softer and turned the color of cinnamon toast. That she's actually pretty cute—like the girl next door come to life.

And I'm still dating her best friend.

The thing is, though I never really admitted it before, maybe I kind of liked that she went to all my hockey games, because, win or lose, she was the one person I could count on to be there no matter what.

Even more than my best friend.
Even more than my girlfriend.

209

Maybe once or twice I've wanted to tell her that, but it just never seemed to be the right time. And so instead it was this unspoken secret the two of us had together.

So maybe I'll tell her today.

I get to her house and her mother leads me around the back. "You're Kelly's boyfriend, aren't you?" she asks, taking a second glance over her shoulder like I'm some player.

I nod, feeling guiltier by the moment, wondering what exactly she knows about my afternoon with her daughter—if she saw all the broken flowers.

Nicole is sitting on the patio with Maria, one of Kelly's friends from school. Maria looks like she's getting ready to leave. She slides her chair back and stands from the table.

That's when Nicole notices me. When her mouth drops open and eyes get wide, like she's gonna freak out.

"Hey," I say, pretty freaked out myself. I mean, what are the odds that Maria would be here, too? I take a deep breath and join them at the table, relieved when Mrs. Bouchard goes back inside the house.

"You're a little late," Maria informs me.

I have no idea what she's talking about. The bug light behind us is zapping up all the bloodthirsty mosquitoes. I almost wish I was one of them. I peek at Nicole, wondering what she's thinking right now—if she absolutely hates me.

"You should have been here an hour ago," Maria

continues, gesturing toward the pile of books on the table—the covers decorated with cakes and streamers.

"Okay," I say, still clueless, wondering why she's being such a bitch—if it's because she knows about what happened this afternoon. I look toward Nicole, trying to figure out if she told her, wondering if either of them said anything to Kelly.

"I got to go," Maria says. "They're gonna be closed by the time I get there."

Good riddance, I feel like saying, but I bite my tongue because Nicole is here.

"Thanks for doing this, Maria," Nicole says. "If they don't have them, we can try Party Central tomorrow."

"What are you shopping for?" I ask.

"Maria's going over to Celebrations before it closes," Nicole explains. "We're on a mission for some Hawaiian leis—the floral ones, not the fuzzy plastic kind."

I nod and it finally clicks; they're planning Kelly's welcome-home party.

As if I could feel any crappier.

Maria rolls her eyes at me, like she's annoyed that I'm even here. Part of me feels bad for the girl. She's had more scores made on her than the touchdown post at our school's football field, but that still doesn't stop her from playing wide receiver.

"What? What are you staring at?" she snaps at me—just out of nowhere.

"Nothing," I snap back.

"Maria's been a *huge* help," Nicole says, intercepting. "She has some really cool ideas."

"Paper streamers and Hawaiian leis don't exactly equal up to *cool* ideas," Maria squawks.

"Whatever," Nicole says. "You forgot to mention the other three thousand brilliant ideas you came up with. The girl should seriously be a party planner."

Maria looks away and yanks down the sleeves of her sweatshirt, like she can't stand to be complimented.

"Wait. I almost forgot," Nicole says, jumping up from the table. "Don't go yet."

Maria lets out this big-ass sigh. "I told you, I have to leave."

Nicole ignores her, running back into the house, emerging from the sliders a few seconds later, gift bag in hand. It's the first time I notice that she's wearing this short peach sundress with the straps of her bathing suit sticking out. When did she get so cute? And why didn't I see it until just this afternoon?

"What's that?" Maria asks.

"I got you a little something," Nicole says, totally beaming at her. "It's nothing, really. Just something I've been holding on to."

"You don't have to buy me stuff," Maria says with another eye-roll. "I told you already. I'm not mad about earlier. I wouldn't even have kept calling you if it wasn't for

Kelly's party. The girl's going to be totally pissed if we don't do it up big."

"No, no—I got this *before* I messed up our plans."

Maria opens the bag, pulling out a black nylon backpack with metallic silver stitching, the letters *CS* written in graffitilike scribbles across the front.

"Cryptic Slaughter," Nicole explains, pointing at the letters. "I ordered it off their Web site."

"Are you serious?" Her bottom lip quivers just a bit, like maybe she's not used to people doing nice things for her.

"To start off the new school year. . . . Like it?"

Maria runs her fabric-covered fingers over the surface, her sleeves pulled down over her hands even though it's ninety frickin' degrees out. A crystal pendant hangs around her neck. Nicole touches it. "Is this new?" she asks.

Maria shrugs. "A friend gave it to me."

"It's pretty on you."

"Thanks," Maria says, her voice barely even audible. She peeks up at Nicole finally, her face all red like she can't say anything else. It's like the words are stuck in her throat—like she's all choked up.

Nicole gives Maria a hug and tells her that she'll pick her up first thing in the morning for breakfast and more party-planning at Red's.

Maria nods me good-bye, her eyes all red and focused toward the ground. And then she leaves.

And then Nicole and I are alone.

Nicole lights the citronella candle in the center of the table and slumps down in her chair, her body angled off toward the yard, her thick rubber-soled sandals only half pulled onto her feet.

"That was really cool of you," I say.

"What do you mean?"

"I mean the backpack. The way you were with her."

She shrugs like it was nothing, like it's just a part of who she is.

"So, we should talk about earlier," I say, grabbing a pretzel from the bowl on the table. "What do you think we should do about it?"

"What do you mean?" She's picking at her fingernails now.

"I mean, Kelly's your best friend."

"And?" She can barely even look at me.

"You didn't talk to her today, did you?"

"No."

"Did you tell Maria?"

She shakes her head, and I'm more than relieved. I let out a breath but then feel like a dick.

"We don't have to say anything if you don't want to," she says, as though reading my mind.

"I know." I shrug. "It's just . . . I don't know. I don't want you to think I'm some jerk or anything."

"So, what *do* you want?"

More shrugging.

"You know what this reminds me of?" she says. "That time in the fourth grade when you told Gina Bailey you'd be her valentine, but instead you gave all your sweetheart candies to Marley Maihos. Gina ended up bawling during recess."

"I can't believe you remember that."

"I remember a lot," she says, looking away—her voice barely above a whisper.

"That was a rough year for me," I say in my own defense.

She nods and looks back at me. "I know. I was *there*, remember?"

"No," I say, shaking my head like she doesn't get it. "There was just some personal stuff that happened— family drama stuff."

"You mean with your parents?"

I feel my face screw up. "How do you know about that?"

Nicole shrugs, telling me how she remembers the essay I wrote in English class—"What I Did During Christmas Vacation"—which sort of turned into "Why My Christmas Sucked Because My Parents Are Going to Get a Divorce." Our ass of a teacher made me read the entire thing aloud in class.

Nicole sits there, detailing the essay like she wrote it herself—like all of this just happened yesterday. She remembers how my dad's work wanted him to transfer to

Ohio, how that caused my mother to freak out since her family is here, and how I was scared out of my mind that they'd end up divorced—since they never really got along anyway.

"I can't believe you remember all that."

"It's why you started working at such a young age, right?"

"Did I tell you that?"

She nods. "In art class. You told me that you wanted to get a job as soon as you could because your father lost his job. I figured it was because he didn't move to Ohio. Didn't you start working at, like, twelve or something?"

I nod, completely blown away by her—by all that she remembers, by how well she seems to know me.

"I really admired that about you," she continues. "That you wanted to help out your family, that you wanted to pitch in and earn a few bucks. I think about it when I'm being really lazy."

"Wow," I say, leaning back in my chair, amazed that someone like her could ever be inspired by someone like me. I mean, nobody thinks of me like that—not even Kelly.

When Kelly said yes to going out with me eight months ago, I was psyched. She's one of those girls you just never think you can get—super hot, kick-ass bod, likes to laugh. The type of girl you imagine hanging on the arm of some jacked-up quarterback with a Porsche 911. Not

that I'm bad. I mean, I consider myself pretty good looking. I work out at least three times a week for hockey and
I'm saving up to buy a Jeep. It's just that, I don't know, I
always thought Kelly was in a different league. And when
we started dating, I felt like people looked at me like I was
in that league, too.

I wonder if that girl I met today at Dunkin' is right,
and Kelly really did go to California to be with someone
else. Would she really cheat on me like that?

Do I even care?

"What happened to your hand?" She's looking at the
gash across the palm. From today, when my garden shears
slipped, because I wasn't paying attention. Just after we . . .
did it. I ended up stopping the bleeding with a rag and I
thought I was all set, but then, on my way home, my car
blew a tire, and the gash completely opened up while I was
trying to put on the spare.

"Landscaping accident," I say, forgoing the lengthy
explanation.

"Why don't you have a bandage on it?"

"I did. I had this scarf-thing on it earlier, but it just
kept coming undone so I ended up taking it off."

Nicole shakes her head and gets up, goes back inside
the house, and a few seconds later, comes out with a first-
aid kit. She rolls my palm open, plunks a peroxide-sopping
wad of cotton in the center, and swipes downward. The
sting burns so bad I almost piss myself. *Major pain!*

"It's gonna sting a little," she says, halfway through the process.

"Just a little," I say, biting the inside of my cheek.

She tosses the cotton to the side, grabs this long white tube, and squeezes a couple wormlike squirts across the wound. "I'm fine," I say. "It's stopped bleeding."

"Yeah, but if you don't want an infection, you need to take care of it." She tops the whole procedure off by covering my hand with gauze and enough medical tape to wrap the gifts of everybody on my Christmas list for the next five years.

"Thanks," I say.

"You're welcome."

"Do you make house calls?"

"I've retired that service," she says.

"That's too bad."

She smiles and then bites her bottom lip like she's trying to hold it in, but the smile is too big and so she just lets it out. "What?" she asks, her face turning red like I've totally embarrassed her.

"Nothing. I don't know."

It's just so weird. In my car, on the way over here, I knew exactly what I wanted to do about this afternoon. I had the words practically memorized—*Nicole, what happened between us was great and I'll always remember it, but for some reason I think we got carried away. It was nobody's fault; it just happened, but I think it was probably a mistake. I'm still with*

Kelly. She's your best friend. I think it's best for all of us if we don't say anything. But now, face-to-face, talking with her like this, watching the shadow of the candle flame flicker against her bottom lip, I don't think I can say any of that.

I don't think I want to, either.

So we end up hanging out for a while, just shooting the shit. Nicole tells me how she wants to take some calligraphy class this fall. And I tell her how I want to try playing goalie this year. We talk about how neither of us has started our summer reading yet and how, if my plan works out, I should have enough money saved up for a semi-new Jeep by Thanksgiving. And it's cool—how the conversation just flows; how she asks me lots of questions and looks into my eyes when I answer, like she's really interested in what I'm saying; not just fake interested the way Kelly is a lot of the time. And so I can't help but ask her, "How come you like me so much?"

She looks off in the direction of the pool, like the question doesn't surprise her one bit—like maybe she's been asked that question a lot. "I don't know," she says finally. "I just do . . . you know?"

I nod, beginning to understand maybe—finally—how truly cool she is. I look over at the flower bed. Mrs. Bouchard's got a spotlight sticking up out of the ground to highlight the garden. But the place is a complete mess. The mulch is everywhere, the lilies are broken, those tall grass-blade things look all mangled. The sight of it makes me laugh. I try to hold it in, but I can't help but laugh like a freaking idiot.

"What?" She's laughing, too.

"Can I ask you a totally random question?"

She nods.

"Who's your papergirl?"

"My *papergirl*?"

"It's stupid, really. It's just, this girl I met today—some freshman I think—told me that your papergirl saw us . . . you know . . . earlier . . . in the garden."

"What?"

"I think she was lying."

"How does she know, then?"

"I don't know. She might've just been bluffing, you know, trying to get me going. She just said her papergirl saw me and some girl; she didn't get all specific about it."

"So it might not even have been me. I don't even *have* a paper*girl*. Frankie Johannesen delivers our newspapers. It must have been some other girl you were with." She looks away again.

"There isn't any other girl," I say.

"Just Kelly," she says.

"Yeah." Kelly. I look away, too.

It's weird though, because half the time I don't even feel like Kelly gives a shit about me. She blows me off, refuses to hang with me at lunch, and sometimes says stuff about me in front of other people that totally pisses me off.

Like, she'll make fun of my car or my landscaping job, or that my nose is crooked from when it got busted last year in hockey. I laugh it off like it's no big deal. Even though it is. Even though I've told her a million times that I hate it.

Right before she left for her dad's, I could sense her pushing me away. I took her out to dinner at this four-star place, bought her the Scallops del Mar—the most expensive thing on the menu—but all she kept saying throughout the whole entire meal was stuff like, "We're going to change so much this summer" and "There's a whole world out there just waiting for us."

All I was trying to tell her was that I'd miss her.

But then other times, it's like she's all into me. Telling me all her problems, telling me how lucky she is to be with a guy like me, jumping into my lap and macking on me like she couldn't be happier about us. It's totally screwed up.

Nicole and I sit in awkward silence for several seconds. I notice the silhouette of Mrs. Bouchard pass by the sliders a couple times, checking up on us. I guess it's getting late, but I don't want to leave, and so I ask her the one question that's been weighing on my mind for a couple months now: "I don't expect you to answer this and I can't even believe I'm asking it, but do you know if Kelly is cheating on me?"

What surprises me most is that her expression doesn't change one bit, doesn't show shock or even a speck of emotion. "Honestly," she says, "I don't know. I don't think so."

"You don't *think* so?"

She shakes her head, and we're quiet for a few seconds. I want to tell her how that girl from Dunkin' told me that Kelly was dating some guy from jail. But maybe I've said enough about Kelly for one night. Maybe this isn't really about Kelly at all. Maybe this is about me and Nicole.

"Did you mean what you said earlier?" she asks.

"What did I say?"

"You know, just before . . . before we went into the garden?"

"We said a lot of things."

She nods and takes a sip of her iced tea, not willing to budge. And so I budge for her. "Do you mean when I said that I may have thought about us, you know, being together?"

"Yeah. Did you mean it?"

Before I can answer, my cell phone starts ringing. I want to ignore it, but I can't because it's just . . . there, breaking the moment, ring after ring.

"Go ahead," Nicole says. "Answer it."

I pull the phone from my pocket and click it on. "Hello?"

"Hi," Kelly says, on the other end.

I cup over the receiver like Nicole can hear. But it's like she doesn't even have to hear, because I can tell she just knows. She looks away, back toward the pool, drinking her iced tea down until her straw makes sucking sounds. "Hi," I say into the phone. "Can I call you back?"

"No," she says. "Where have you been all day?"

The reflection of the moon is back-floating across the surface of the pool, making me want to jump right in. I wonder if Nicole is thinking the same thing.

"Hel-looo?" Kelly calls from the receiver. "Are you *there*?"

"Yeah," I say, wondering how long she's been trying to get my attention.

"I've been trying to call you all day," she says. "Your cell phone kept going to voice mail."

"Oh. I must have had it turned off."

"I'm coming home."

"What do you mean?"

"I mean I hate it here. I don't know why I came. I miss you. I want to come home. I want to see you."

"What's wrong? Did something happen?"

Nicole gets up and heads toward the sliders. I try to signal her, but it's like she's purposely ignoring me. "Nicole," I shout out, before she can close the door behind her.

"Nicole?" I hear on the other end of the phone.

Nicole turns around.

"Where are you going?" I ask her.

Nicole jiggles her empty glass, just the ice cubes shifting around at the bottom, then closes the slider.

"Is Nickie with you?" Kelly asks.

"Yeah."

"Wait," she says, her voice lighting up. "You guys aren't planning something for me, are you?"

"You guessed it," I say, letting out a breath, reminding myself how screwed I am.

"Why are you so sweet?" she bursts. "I never should have left you this summer."

Nicole emerges from the sliders again, a turquoise shawl draped over shoulders, and two fresh glasses of iced tea—one for me, which she clunks down on the table.

"My flight should get in to Logan around three A.M." Kelly says.

"Tonight?"

"Well, tomorrow morning, technically. I'm taking the red-eye. I'm at the airport right now; I just up and left. It's not like anybody at my dad's will even notice."

"Are you okay?"

"I'm fine," she snaps, like she's annoyed that I'm asking again. "So will you pick me up?"

"Is she okay?" Nicole whispers at me.

I give a slight nod, watching as she settles into the porch swing—her sandals off, bare feet up, using the shawl as a blanket to cover her legs.

"I have to be to work by six tomorrow morning," I tell her. "Can I call the shuttle service for you? They pick you up right at your terminal and bring you home."

"*What?* I book an emergency flight home just to be with you and you tell me to take a shuttle bus? Are you kidding me?"

"I'm sorry," I say. "It's just . . . I'm gonna get fired if I show up late again."

"Tell her I'll pick her up," Nicole says, obviously catching the gist of the conversation.

"No!" Kelly shouts in my ear, having heard Nicole's voice. "I want YOU to pick me up."

"I'm sorry, Kelly. I told you, I have to be to work by six."

"But—"

"Listen," I say. "Why don't you give me a ring tomorrow, let me know you got in okay. I've got to go—I've got something I gotta take care of." I look over at Nicole, and she smiles at me. I smile, too, wondering if she'd mind if I kissed her tonight.

"What could be more important than me?" Kelly asks.

"Tomorrow, okay?"

I click the phone off, order Kelly her shuttle, and then join Nicole over on the porch swing—exactly where I belong.

Acknowledgments

I first want to thank fellow Emersonians and members of my writers' group, Lara Zeises, Tea Benduhn, and Steven Goldman, who were with me through every word of this novel. Many, many thanks for your friendship, support, and encouragement. I am a better writer because of it.

Thanks to Kathryn Green, my agent extraordinaire, who continues to offer fabulous advice and constructive feedback, and who helped make this happen. I am forever grateful.

Thanks to my editors, Alessandra Balzer and Jennifer Besser, for their warmth, sense of humor, and editorial brilliance.

A special thanks to my former writing teacher Steve Almond, who first read Nicole's story in a fiction writing class at Emerson College, and who encouraged me to create this collection.

I'm lucky to have so many friends and family members in my corner—you know who you are. A special thanks to my mother (my biggest fan), to Ryan, Mark, Neil, Lee, Laurie, and MaryKay. And to Ed, who has read all my work—in all its many stages—at least a hundred times. Thank you for your continuous love, support, and friendship.

Thanks to Michael Faria for his Game Boy expertise and to Delia Faria, Haig Demarjian, and fellow Emersonian Kim Ablon Whitney for reading pieces of *Bleed* and offering feedback.

And finally, a great big thank-you goes to my readers, who continue to support me and cheer me on. Your continuous encouragement makes all the difference. Thank you so much!